Best wishes Bob —

Bitter End Trail

Here's hoping you enjoy
my stories of the
Southwest trails series.
Thank you for following
my novellas.

As ever,
Diane

Also by DIANE M. CECE

Book 1: *Trails Southwest*

Book 2: *The Cattle Drive from Southwest*

Book 3: *The Rodeo Southwest*

Book 4: *Whispering Ridge*

Available from Xlibris LLC

Bitter End Trail

Book 5 in the Southwest Series

Diane M. Cece

Diane M. Cece

To order additional copies of this book, contact:
Xlibris
1-888-795-4274
www.Xlibris.com
Orders@Xlibris.com
710681

CONTENTS

DEDICATION

For all veterans and my family of law enforcement officers,
Laura Barbato, NYPD, and Louis Barbato,
retired chief of police, New Jersey.
Also, for my dear friend retired officer Walt
Sevensky, Mt Olive Police, NJ.

My "thank-you" seems so small compared to all you've done for America and the citizens of New York and New Jersey. It's a comfort to know our veterans and our law enforcement officers can protect us from the twenty-first-century outlaw.

ACKNOWLEDGMENTS

The author would like to take this opportunity to thank several individuals without whose assistance, this series could not have been possible.

Thank you, Mary Flores, publishing consultant; Michael Green, submissions representative; Lorie Adams and Clifford Young, author services representatives; James Colonia, Lloyd Griffith, Cynthia Mathews, Marie Giles, Lorraine Cariete, Ryan Cortes, and Neil Reid, manuscript services representatives; David Castro, Ronald Flor, Jane Javier, Marly Trent, Orlando Wade, Heidi White, Monica Williams, marketing service representatives; Tony Hermano, author consultant; Lloyd Baron, web design; Amerie Evans, senior book consultant; Chad Pitt, marketing consultant; Mark Anthony Bao, cover image and Leo Montano, customer services.

Thank you, John Covert, 27thnewjerseycompanyf.org for designing my website, dianesoldwestnovels.com. John, you have been a tremendous inspiration for getting this author technologically advanced.

Thanks again, everyone, for being a part of my life and my work. You are the best ever that anyone can have available at their right side as colleagues and friends.

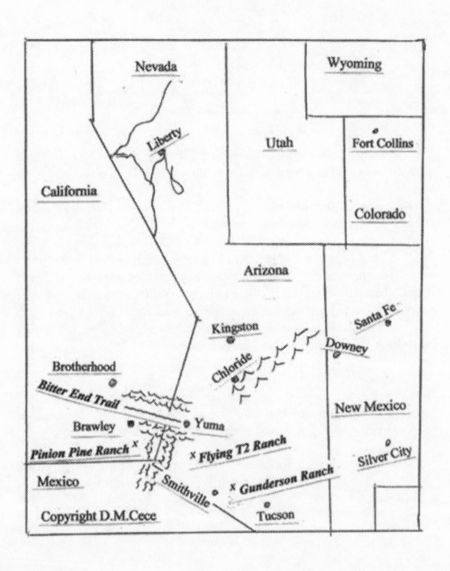

The Nevada Kid
Family Tree

Thomas Lacey   and   Polly Trainor
1851   1851–1882

|
|

Thomas Junior "TJ" Trainor
1872

Thomas Lacey   married   Recordina Raucci
1851   1858

|
|

Thomas "TJ" Lacey
1872 (Adopted 1882)

Cimarron Lacey
1882

Tyler "Ty" Lacey
1883

Sundell Lacey
1884

Gage Lacey
1886

Chapter I

ODORIFEROUS RANCH WORK

Arizona, Fall of the Year

I'm called the Cimarron Kid. Don't let that scare you; I picked up the "Kid" handle while I was growing up in the Yuma, Arizona, territory. I'm the second-born son of the notorious outlaw and gunman, the Nevada Kid. My father ran with the Younger Brothers Gang, but after his seven years in Yuma prison, he got a little smarter and went straight and got married to my mother, Ricki, a rodeo barrel racer.

My half brother, Thomas Junior, called TJ for short, is ten years older than me. TJ went to college back East and became an attorney. He is living on the ranch next to ours because, you see, his Great-Uncle John O'Connor, uncle to TJ's mother, Polly Trainor, died of natural causes and left him the ranch next door and the house in his will. He also requested that TJ take care of Aunt Martha. Pa and TJ combined the two ranches and named the big spread the Flying T2 Roughstock and Cattle Company. We raise cattle for the beef industry and roughstock for the rodeo circuit. My Pa jokingly considers me to be part of the roughstock on the ranch. I was born and bred cowboy tough.

My gun is a lot faster than TJ's and probably even faster than my Pa's ever was, but TJ is no wimp. He shoots accurately and can handle a gun almost as good as me, but then again, I had more time to practice speed.

I always try to be a man of honor with clean hands, to do the right thing; however, it don't always turn out that way. Pa wanted me to go back East to college, but I didn't want to go because I love horses better 'n anything. If I went to college, I probably would have picked beer and wimmen as my field of study. You see, I'm actually a chip off the old block. My favorite things are wild horses, beer, and wimmen in that order. Oh yeah, and I love riding roughstock. Pa always said, "When Cimarron is not making dust, he's eating it!"

There are five of us brothers living and growing up on the combined ranches, with TJ being the oldest. I'm twenty, a year older than Tyler, who we call Ty. Sundell is a year younger than Ty, and Gage is two years younger than Sundell. Don't get on the wrong side of any one of us because the five of us brothers together is a force to be reckoned with. Especially me. I have Pa's ball-of-fire personality and badass attitude. As they say, the apple doesn't fall far from the tree. All five of us have Cherokee Indian blood in us from our father's side. The only people I trust are Pa and myself. My Pa always said, "Don't even trust any of your brothers." My Pa was a very smart man, you see.

I'm on my way to Brawley, California, to deliver an order of two roughstock horses and five cinch straps to Jesse Russell at the Pinion Pine Ranch. When it comes to cinch straps, Pa makes the very best. He taught me all he knew, and no one can match the work I do in the tack shop. Brawley is seventy miles west of our Flying T2 Ranch.

Six days on the trail made me dusty and dirty. I could smell my own stink, and I smelled like the horses I was leading. I sent a telegram ahead for a room and a bath at the Cattle Call Hotel, and I couldn't wait to get there at the end of this week. The Bitter End Trail is a dusty, dirty, and stony route to take, but it is the fastest way I know to get where I am going. The trailway is hard, pitiless, and unfeeling to the horses' hooves. It seems like the atmosphere is suddenly showing a disturbance made up by an oncoming storm, possibly an early-winter snow flurry or maybe just thunder and lightning, accompanied by a strong wind. If I leave my slicker off, maybe the rain will wash away some of my trail stink, since I have been offending myself for the last two miles. Oh well, the storm just passed over me, and that slight drizzle was not enough to wash the dust off.

The trail had opened up in front of me, and I came out onto an open plain, and in front of me, I witnessed the robbery of a stagecoach going down. I tied my horses to a small tree and set down my gear. Gotta check the rounds in my gun, do a quick flying mount on Whiskey, and take off toward the stagecoach. I pulled my Winchester from its scabbard as I pushed my knees into Whiskey for a flying takeoff toward the stagecoach. I started firing at the outlaws. I could not save the payroll or the mail, and the outlaws got away when they saw me coming and shooting lead at them. I did manage to hit one of them, wounding him in the arm. I dismounted, climbed up onto the stage, and checked the shotgun guard and the driver; they were both dead. As I climbed down from the driver's seat, a passenger was coming out of the stagecoach door. Oh no! Just what I needed right now. I'm getting stuck with the responsibility of a woman—a good-looking young woman, matter of fact.

"Are you okay, ma'am?"

"Why, yes, I am, mister," she said.

"Are you headed for Brawley, ma'am?"

"Yes. I was visiting friends in Arizona, and my father is expecting me back today. He is meeting me at the stage depot."

"Well, ma'am, the driver and guard are dead. I will have to put them inside the stagecoach. That sign says it's about another fifteen miles yet to town. If you don't mind sitting on the top seat next to me, I can drive the stage for the rest of the way into town. I don't know how else to do this."

"Well, I guess it will have to be all right, cowboy." She got a whiff of him and, at that moment, was not sure she made the right decision. He didn't seem to notice her look of discomfort. She wondered if sitting with the bodies inside the coach would offend her less. She doubted it but had no intention of riding with dead bodies.

"Wait here. I left my horses and gear at the edge of the trail. I'll get them and be right back." When I came back, I tied my roughstock horses and Whiskey to the back of the stagecoach, then put my gear, rigging, and saddle on top of the stagecoach. One at a time, I carried down the two dead men, placing them inside the stage. Then I helped the girl get up into the driver's seat.

All the lady could think of was *This cowboy stinks to high heaven! He smells like a horse. The worse part about it is, he knows it, and it doesn't seem to bother him in the least. How am I going to survive riding fifteen miles next to this awful, offensive stench? Maybe I should keep telling myself it's the safest way for me to get back into town. At least he seemed to be proficient with handling a gun and is not afraid to confront outlaws.*

When I climbed up into the driver's seat, that's when I noticed how very pretty this girl was and that she was not wearing a wedding ring. I knew right then I was in big trouble. *Shit. I smell like my wild horses, haven't had a bath in a week. I am totally aware of my offensive condition and don't have the means to do anything about it. Hope she doesn't object to the scent of horses on a man.*

I slapped rein, and the stage took off with a jolt. I was careful enough to drive it at an easy pace since it was the first time I ever took the reins on a stagecoach. I most certainly didn't want to topple the girl off the high seat. After all, I was towing two wild horses on the back of it also. I never said a word until the lady broke the silence first.

"Thank you for helping me out. What is your name, cowboy?"

"My name is Cimarron, ma'am. What's your name?"

"My name is Janice. I don't ever remember seeing you around Brawley before."

"No, ma'am. It's my first trip to this here town. I'm here on business. My family owns a spread outside of Yuma. We are stock contractors."

"Oh. No wonder."

"No wonder what, ma'am?" I replied when I glanced her way.

"Well, cowboy, what I meant is, you have a distinct animal scent about you much like a cowhand or drover. You don't exactly smell like a barbershop. At first, I thought perhaps you were afraid of water. I know you are not afraid of outlaws."

"I didn't mean to offend you, ma'am, but I've been on the trail, working these wild horses for a week now, and I'm not about to apologize for the way that I am."

"Suit yourself, cowboy. Just get me safely to town as fast as you can."

"It's Cimarron, ma'am. My name is Cimarron Lacey. Call me Cimarron please, Janice."

"Okay, Cimarron. I'll call you Cimarron. If that's what you would like."

"Thank you kindly, ma'am," I said. *There is nothing worse than being attracted to a beautiful woman who is arrogant and can't accept you for the way that you are. I can't wait to get her to Brawley and drop her butt at the stage depot and get on with my business. I hope the saloon girls in Brawley have a better attitude and disposition than this uppity chick.*

It was an hour later when I pulled the stagecoach up in front of the stage depot. Everyone came running up to the stage to see what had happened. I excused myself as I passed in front of Janice and jumped down to help her down from the stage. I did notice she turned her head to the other way and covered the bottom half of her face as I crossed in front of her. The ranch foreman, James was his name, was there to pick her up and take her home, and he seemed to find it very amusing that she turned her face away from me. His giggle was quite obvious. Sheriff Williams came out of his office and approached Janice and me.

"What happened?" asked Sheriff Williams.

"Your stage was robbed, sheriff," I said. "I was coming out of the Bitter End Trail when I saw the outlaws robbing the stage on the road to town, about fifteen miles out, right near that road sign. I'd tried to stop them, but I was too late. I wounded one of them in the arm, sheriff. They got away with the mail and the payroll. The only thing I could do was bring Miss Janice for the rest of the way into town. You'll find the driver and guard inside the stage."

"Are you all right, Janice?" inquired Sheriff Williams.

"Yes, I am, sheriff. I'm fine, except for a nauseous stomach. Guess I could use a little fresh air." I gave Janice my look of disapproval to her last statement. I refuse to be embarrassed by her insults. After all, I did rescue her. My stock horses tied to the back of the stage started to become noisy and restless, pulling at the harnesses and rearing up.

"Hey. Stay away from those two stallions. They are wild," I hollered. The crowd quickly backed away from the horses.

"Hey, sheriff, don't forget, your stage driver and shotgun guard are inside the stage. I didn't want to leave them out on the road."

"You boys get them out and take them down to the undertaker's office," said the sheriff as he pointed into the gathering crowd.

"Who are you, stranger?" said the sheriff.

"My name's Cimarron Lacey. I'm from Yuma, and I have business here in town with these two horses, sheriff. I work at the Flying T2 Roughstock and Cattle Ranch. We are stock contractors."

"I've heard of that ranch. Tom Lacey, the Nevada Kid, owns that spread, if I'm right. I had a poster on him some years ago, until they caught him, tried him, and he did his time."

"That's right, sheriff. I'm one of his sons."

"How many sons does the Kid have?" inquired the sheriff. "I heard he adopted his son, Thomas Trainor. That trial headlined some of the Arizona papers."

"I'm number two of five sons, sheriff."

"Wow! Five sons? That Nevada Kid's been busy producing a lot more than livestock. He only had that ranch for about six years." The sheriff and the crowd that had gathered giggled. I didn't answer. I didn't think it was a very funny comment at all.

"Okay, Cimarron," said the sheriff. "Put your horses up in the corral next to the blacksmith shop and livery before somebody gets too close to them and gets hurt.

Stop by my office and sign my report as a witness to the robbery when you get a chance."

"Sure can, sheriff."

I walked over to the horses, untied the two stallions and my gelding, Whiskey, and walked them over to the livery, putting them into the corral. Looking down the main street of town, I spotted the Cattle Call Hotel and headed directly over to it. I walked up to the desk and checked in.

"I'm Cimarron Lacey. Where can I get a hot bath, a shave, and a haircut? I did telegraph ahead, you know."

"Yes, sir, Mr. Lacey. You do indeed need that bath. I've been wonderin' what time you would show up today," said the hotel clerk. "I'll have a tub and hot water brought up to your room right away. As for the shave and haircut, the barbershop is across the street, mister."

"Thanks," I said. *I'm getting a little tired of the people in this town telling me I need a bath. Maybe I should stay dirty the whole time I'm in town and give them a good reason for getting all riled up! That will show them how much sand I got in my craw. It would keep 'em all away from me too.*

"Charlie. Bring a tub and hot water up to room 10 on the second floor," hollered the desk clerk.

"Make sure that water is good and hot, Charlie," I called out.

"Here is your key, sir. I'll have to charge you fifty cents for the hot water. I'll put it on your bill, Mr. Lacey—and, Mr. Lacey, don't go shooting any holes in that bathtub if the water ain't hot enough. It cost me twelve dollars and twenty-nine cents for a new one after that last cattle drive hit town." *This clerk is a fucking baboon,* I thought.

"Okay, thanks," I said, trying to ignore this peckerwood's last statement. I took my gear upstairs and began unpacking. Thank goodness I didn't lose the bill of sale for the horses. I will make sure Jesse Russell signs it. My brother, TJ, would be pissed off if I don't come home with a signed bill of sale for the ranch ledger. He would kick my butt so hard my belt buckle would wind up around my neck! That ledger would be TJ's problem anyway; I hate bookwork. Busting broncs and eatin' dirt is a lot more fun.

~~~*T2*~~~

The bathtub came and then the hot water. Cimarron undressed and climbed into the tub. *Wow, does this hot water feel good!* he thought. He soaked in it for an hour until his skin began to get wrinkled up. He hated to get out of that tub, but he needed to get on some clean clothes and get over to the barbershop. From his gear bag, he selected his favorite blue Western shirt, with his black leather vest, made from the finest kid leather, and a fresh, rather new, pair of jeans. He wore a silver chain hanging down around his neck, with an Indian arrowhead balanced on the end of it. The arrowhead was made out of pure silver. This chain and arrowhead easily caught one's eye because only three shirt buttons were snapped at the bottom of the shirt, exposing some of his upper chest. The dark curly chest hair made a soft bed for the arrowhead to rest on. The background of dark hair accented the silver, making it stand out as sharper and more noticeable against his chest. His boots were made of snakeskin, very different from the muddy, manure-caked work boots and dusty, leather-fringed chaps he wore on the trail. When he descended from the stairs and came into the lobby, the desk clerk noticed a significant difference of appearance in the man. The man was actually very good-looking and younger-looking than what the clerk first thought.

~~~T2~~~

I left the hotel and crossed the street to the barbershop. "I need a shave, and trim my hair too," I said.

"Shaves are ten cents, and haircuts are fifteen cents," said the proprietor.

"Fine," I said.

A close, clean, razor-sharp shave and a trim to even up my shaggy hair would give me that polished look of a successful rancher, as Pa would say.

Now all I need is some supper, a drink at the saloon, and some evening entertainment, and I will be all set. Tomorrow, I will deliver the horses and cinch straps to the Flying T2's new client and then take my time going back home. Another job well done.

I paid the barber and left the shop. I headed straight for the sheriff's office. When I entered, I could smell fresh coffee brewing.

"That paperwork ready yet, sheriff?"

"Yes, it is, young man. Sign right here on the bottom after you read it and make sure I wrote it up exactly the way you described it."

I read the report and signed it. "That coffee smells good. See you later, sheriff. I'm hungry and need something to eat."

"Try the café five doors down. The food is good there," said Sheriff Williams.

"Thanks, sheriff."

I headed down to the café for a steak dinner. I was tired of my own campfire cooking and eating small bits of wild game out on the trail. A beer with my meal washed down the trail dust in my throat. The waitress was coming on to me and flirting.

This is much better. Things are finally getting back to normal for me after all the insults and nonsense about my offensive, stinking hide.

I paid the bill, leaving a nice tip, winked at her, tipping my hat, and went on down the boardwalk to the Branding Iron Saloon & Dance Hall. I ordered a drink of whiskey, drank it down fast to relax myself, then ordered another, taking my time with the second drink. A couple of saloon girls started hanging around me and flirting with me. I looked them both over and put my arm around the one I felt most attracted to, pulling her in against me. The other girl got the hint as to my interest and walked away.

"How about a drink with me, ma'am?"

"I'd love it, handsome. Where did you blow in from tumbleweed?"

"I came across from Yuma. I have business in town to take care of tomorrow."

"How long you staying, cowboy?

"My name's Cimarron, ma'am. My friends call me the Cimarron Kid. I'm staying for as long as it takes to get my business done."

"You got any business going on tonight, Cimarron Kid? My name is Jennifer."

"Actually, I don't. I got a free night in town tonight, thank you for asking, ma'am. Why? You got something else in mind?"

Cimarron gave her his contagious winning smile. The Kid possessed the knack to eyeball a saloon girl from across the room and pick out just the right one that would offer him a trick. Piano music was playing in the saloon, and a couple of cowhands were dancing with the other saloon girls.

"First, we will have this dance. Then you can buy a bottle, and we'll go upstairs to my room. How does that sound, Cimarron?" she asked.

"Sweetheart, that sounds like a well-thought-out plan to me, especially after the way I've been treated today."

"Someone's been treating you poorly, honey?"

"Let's just say this town needs a better welcoming committee and let it go at that."

I offered her my hand and walked her out onto the dance floor. I took her in my arms, holding her tight against the length of me, so I could feel every womanly curve, and we did the two-step around the dance floor. As others joined us on the floor and began crowding me in, tipping over and bumping against me, I decided I'd had enough and quit dancing, bought a bottle at the bar, and led Jennifer toward the stairs. Jennifer pushed in front of me, taking the lead, and showed me to her room.

~~~T2~~~

I slept late the next morning, having come in at an early hour from the saloon and Jennifer's room. I was satisfied and relaxed and feeling free like a raven on the wing. I didn't care much about what time it was when I got up and dressed for breakfast.

That Jennifer wore me out. I rode broncs and uncorked stallions in less time than it took to tame her down. Maybe I should go back there and see her again tonight. At least somebody in this town likes me and wants to have some fun.

I'll get up and quickly dress since it's already late morning. The two stallions need to be fed, looked after, and delivered to the Pinion Pine

Ranch, and I need to pick up the money and get a signature from Jesse Russell on this here paper for TJ.

I decided to take care of my business before I got distracted into doing anything else. I could just hear TJ now, scolding me for not getting the job done right. TJ could not only scold me, his younger brother, with as much cusswords as would peel the skin off a Gila monster, but then he would deck me with his right fist, and God made pain hurt bad. TJ was like Pa, you see; he had a temper he couldn't control. The more I thought about being decked by my older brother TJ, the more anxious I was to get the job done and the horses delivered safely to their destination.

On my way down to the corral and livery, I stopped by the general store to pick up genuine Bull Durham loose-leaf chewing tobacco, more jerky, and a few supplies for the trail back in the morning. Chewing and spitting would keep me occupied on the trail back home, especially if I was to daydream with thoughts of the good time I'd had with Jennifer. I couldn't wait to get back and tell Ty, Sundell, and Gage about her. Those boys love to hear my adventure stories.

While walking toward the corral and livery stable, I noticed someone was messing around with one of my prize stallions. I broke into a run toward the corral and quickly climbed the fence.

"Hey, mister. Just what the fuck you think you are trying to do with my horse?"

"I was just trying to teach him a lesson and quiet him down a little. He was making a lot of noise, acting wild."

"Quiet him down by smacking him with a fucking horse whip? If you put one mark on this animal, I'll whip *you* with that thing, you son of a bitch. This animal belongs to the Pinion Pine Ranch," I said, "and I don't intend to bring him there as damaged goods."

Sheriff Williams was coming up the street now to see what all the commotion was about down by the livery stable.

"Well, maybe you should have been here earlier this morning to feed and take proper care of him, you stinkin', lazy, horse wrangler," replied the roughneck cowhand. "Maybe he wouldn't be makin' so much noise, disturbing the whole town."

"Maybe you should be mindin' your own damn business, smart-ass," I said.

"I don't like the way you talk, stranger. Maybe this needs settling here and now. I think you ought to go for your gun! You draw first, wiseass."

"No," I said. "I'm not a gunfighter. I only draw in self-defense, you prick." The sheriff arrived at the corral just in time to hear my last words.

"Well then, I'll settle this fast, you coward," the cowhand drew first and fired, missing me high when I drew faster and killed him point-blank.

The sheriff climbed in through the fence, pushing past me, kneeling down, and checking the dead cowboy.

"It's Dave Spence, and he is dead."

"Aw, shit," I said. "Sheriff, it was self-defense. I swear it. It was self-defense."

"I know it was, Cimarron. I saw and heard some of it as I was running up to the corral. Did you have to kill him? Why couldn't you just shoot the gun out of his hand?"

"It happened too fast, sheriff. I'm a defensive shooter. Am I under arrest?"

"You should be, mister. But I'm not gonna arrest you because I'm a witness, and I saw and heard some of it. Young man, you get these horses out of town and delivered and get out of my town. I don't want to see your face around Brawley after tomorrow, Kid. Understand?"

"Yes, sir. I'll leave as soon as I finish with my business, sheriff." I turned and gathered up the stallions to calm them down. When they settled, I saddled Whiskey, mounted, and led the wild horses out of town.

Sheriff Williams had a couple of men remove Dave Spence's body from the corral and take it to the undertaker. He said Dave's brother would have to be notified. *Just what I needed,* I thought when I heard that. Dave Spence had relatives. Shit.

~~~T2~~~

It was noontime when I reached the Pinion Pine Ranch, and I was greeted at the gate by James, the ranch foreman. James opened the gate and directed me to take the horses to the large corral to the left side of the main ranch house. James went into the house and came out with Jesse Russell. Jesse was excited to see his stallions, as was several of his cowhands, who were now rushing over to the corral to get a look at the new animals.

"Thanks for bringing them, son," said Jesse Russell.

I offered him my hand to shake, and as we were shaking hands, I said, "My name is Cimarron Lacey, sir. My friends call me the Cimarron Kid."

"Are you the Nevada Kid's son?" asked Jesse.

"Yes, sir. I'm one of them."

"Boy, do you look exactly like your father, a spittin' image of him in his younger days. How is the Nevada Kid doing? He was a ball of fire when I knew him."

"He is doing good, sir, aging a little, and he has his hands full, raising us five boys and trying to keep up with us."

"I don't doubt that, with his own bloodline in you, and he deserves every bit of aggravation that y'all can give him." Jesse laughed loudly.

"I have a paper for you to sign for receiving the horses and five cinch straps, fulfilling your agreement with our Flying T2 Ranch," I replied.

"Sure. C'mon up to my office in the house, and I'll pay you cash for the delivery."

I followed Jesse Russell up to the ranch house, and we went into his office. Jesse gave me one thousand, five hundred dollars in cash, and I put it in my leather money belt around my waist.

"I'm having a late lunch today, Cimarron. Stay and have lunch with me and my daughter," said Jesse.

"I'll take you up on that offer, sir. I missed breakfast and haven't eaten lunch yet. I'm very beholden to you for the offer, sir. I never turn down a home-cooked meal."

"You're welcome, Cimarron. Your pa raises good livestock on that ranch."

We went into the dining room and sat down. Jesse passed glasses of brandy to sip with our lunch. His daughter, Janice, walked in with a tray full of sandwiches, homemade soup, and some fresh, homemade potato salad, with slices of hot apple pie for dessert. I did a double take when she walked in through the dining room door, and I almost fell off the chair as I choked on my drink. Janice saw me at the same instant and almost dropped the tray of sandwiches, soup, potato salad, and dessert all over the floor. The soup spilled a little on the tray.

"Are you all right, son?" inquired Jesse. "My gosh, Janice. Are you okay also?

"Sure am, Pa. Guess I tripped on the rug."

Jesse turned and looked at me for some kind of an answer.

"Yes, sir. The brandy went down my Sunday throat, as my Ma would say. So sorry, sir. Ahem." I tried clearing my throat again so I could speak clearly. "Ahem. Janice! Is this where you live? Are you Jesse's daughter?"

"I most certainly am, cowboy. So I see those horses you were bringing in were actually for my father."

"Yes, ma'am," I replied.

"You two know each other?" inquired Jesse Russell.

"Father, this is the young man I told you *all* about that saved my life and brought me in on the stage."

Jesse started laughing. *So this is the cowboy that had what Janice called the rank-horse stink on him,* he thought.

"Cimarron, you sure do look different in more ways than one. May I say you clean up well. By that strong fragrance you are wearing, I can see you took my advice about splashing in some water, and you even stopped at the barbershop for a clean shave and some scent."

"It wasn't just because of you, Miss Janice. It was something I would do anyway."

"Is that right, cowboy? Well, I'm glad you did it sooner rather than later."

"Yes, ma'am." I was feeling rather shy and embarrassed. "Jesse, maybe I better have lunch in town. I'm not so sure your daughter wants me here."

"Don't be silly, Cimarron. She'll get over it! You are my guest. Janice, sit down and behave yourself. This man is our guest for lunch. He is the son of a good friend of mine, the Nevada Kid, from Yuma, Arizona. The Cimarron Kid is a rancher, like myself. You know how dirty and filthy ranch work can be. You certainly washed and patched enough of my clothes to know what it's all about."

I had a smirk on my face. *It's about time somebody put this spoiled chick in her place,* I thought. *Who better than her father?* Janice just scowled at both of us and sat down at the table to join us for lunch.

"I'm sorry, Cimarron. I guess I made a mistake and overreacted toward you on the stage ride into town. I didn't know you had business with my father. You didn't say that." Janice was having second thoughts about this cowboy. He was not just attractive with the layers of dirt and stink washed off him, but he was a siren of seductive temptation to any young woman. Clean-shaven, tousled hair combed out, and dressed up, he certainly looked like a successful and rich young rancher. She was feeling embarrassed that her harsh words abused him the way they did.

"Apology accepted, ma'am." I politely tipped my hat to her.

He even accepted my apology with an air of class and a nice smile, Janice thought. "Is that an Indian arrowhead you are wearing around your neck?" she queried.

"Yes, ma'am, Miss Janice. I have Cherokee Indian blood in me on my father's side. My mother gave me this neck chain. The arrowhead is made of pure silver."

"Wow. That is very rich-looking. I'm very impressed." Janice realized that that arrowhead sitting on his chest between two very strong, muscular-looking shoulders would entice any girl to sink into his chest and have him wrap those strong arms tightly around her so she could get lost in him.

"Thank you, ma'am," I said. We finished the noon meal. Then I stood up from the table. "Thank you for lunch, Miss Janice and Mr. Russell. I guess I'll be going now."

"Wait a minute, son. How about another brandy? Are you going back to Yuma right away?"

"Well, I planned on leaving around noon tomorrow, sir. As for another round, no thanks, sir." *I had it in the back of my mind to stop by Jennifer's room again tonight for more fun. Noontime would probably be the earliest I could get to pack and shove off for home.*

"I would like you to come by and have dinner with us tonight. Some of the boys are going to try breaking these stallions tonight. Don't you want to be here for the fun? You don't have anything else to do for tonight, do you, Cimarron?"

I hesitated and glanced at Janice. "Uh, no, I guess not, sir. Sure, I'll stop by. What time?"

"How does around six o'clock sound?"

I checked my pocket watch. "Okay, sir. See you then." *Maybe I can see Jennifer later,* I thought. Mounting Whiskey, I headed back to Brawley.

~~~T2~~~

I stopped by the telegraph office and sent a message to my brother, TJ, and my Pa, telling them that the two stallions and five cinches were delivered and that I had the cash on me in my leather money belt. I told them that the agreement was signed and was in my shirt pocket and that I would be home in a week and that I was taking the Bitter End Trail back since I found that to be the fastest way to travel from Brawley to Yuma. I neglected to tell them about the little bit of trouble I had earlier in town. No sense in making them worry over something since I wasn't under arrest. I was just ordered out of town, which was really no big deal. It's happened before to me.

Around six o'clock that evening, I enjoyed a delicious rare steak with Janice and her father, Jesse Russell. I appreciated a good home-cooked meal, and Janice was not a bad cook. After dinner, I watched the wranglers try their best to take the pitch out of the stallions I brought to Jesse. They even let me have a turn on one of them to show them how I do it. Of course, I ate dirt again, trying to show off for Janice.

After brushing off my good clothes and rubbing my hand over the bruises and sore spots, Janice decided we should sit on the porch swing for a while as it was a beautiful starry evening. We sat and talked for about fifteen minutes, pointing out the constellations like Orion and the Big Dipper, when I noticed a good-looking, well-cared-for guitar leaning against the clapboards of the house. I picked up the guitar and tuned it up tight. A love song at this moment would make a perfect romantic setting for this beautiful evening. I began to sing "San Antonio Rose," using the skills my pa taught me for the acoustic-guitar accompaniment. Pa taught all of us boys to play the guitar and sing. It was something he liked to do all the time. My youngest brother, Gage, played the harmonica. Ma loved it when Pa sang, and when all five of us boys started playing and singing in harmony all together with Pa, the whole Flying T2 spread would sway to the rhythm of the music. Janice was quite overwhelmed with the love songs I sang, and I think my singing won her over a bit. I gently placed the guitar back where I found it and told her I needed to leave.

"Well, ma'am, I'm gonna say good night to y'all now. I got to pack my roll and make the trip back to Yuma tomorrow. It was nice meetin' ya. Maybe someday, I'll drift back here again."

"I hope it's soon, Cimarron. I enjoyed your singing."

"You never can tell when I'll show up, ma'am. I'm a drifter. When I'm not working on the Flying T2 spread, I'm delivering the stock orders all over the countryside. I drift in and out of places on short notice, and I never stay for very long. I just hope the next time we encounter each other, it will be under sweeter, more fragrant circumstances!" I giggled, proud of my own joke. "So long, miss." I tipped my hat to Janice and headed across the yard to my horse, Whiskey.

Now Janice was feeling slightly embarrassed by the way she treated him after listening to a farewell like that from this hot-looking cowboy. *Under sweeter, more fragrant circumstances,* she thought. *Darn it. That good-looking cowboy will probably never forget how I put him down. Me and my clumsy blundering luck.*

~~~T2~~~

As I rode out, I was thinking I really needed to leave early, fully knowing there was no more time for messing around with Jennifer at the saloon, because I wanted to get an early start first thing in the morning. Going back to the saloon with this much money in my money belt was not a very good idea. My brother, TJ, would be so proud of me making an intelligent decision such as that. Maybe I'm actually beginning to make decisions to his liking.

When I got back to the Cattle Call Hotel, I paid my bill and told the clerk that I was leaving very early in the morning. He probably wouldn't be up when I left. The problem began when I entered my room and found that it had been ransacked. Someone was looking for something and did not find what they were looking for. Could it be that someone was looking for my money belt that I had on me all the time? Maybe the telegraph clerk shared my telegram with someone other than my family. It also could have been friends or relatives of that roughneck cowboy I shot down at the corral this morning. Were they looking for me? Whatever someone's problem was, I went immediately downstairs and out the door to the sheriff's office. I reported the ransacked room to the sheriff, and he made out a report. I signed a complaint form. The sheriff went back to the room with me and checked it for evidence. The only thing he found was the mess.

Since this interruption upset my applecart, I decided to stop by the Branding Iron Saloon & Dance Hall and say my good-byes to Jennifer before I retired for bed. The saloon was very busy and noisy as I entered, and Jennifer spotted me the moment I entered through the batwing doors. She came right up to me and gave me a big hug and a kiss. I explained to her that I was leaving in the morning and that I was just here to say good-bye to her and that I was not staying with her for the night. We sat down at a round table in the corner and enjoyed a drink together and some quiet conversation. It wasn't helping me one bit when she put her hand on my thigh and kept rubbing it back and forth, getting a little higher with each stroke. Boy, did she have a nice touch. I was being tempted and pressured into staying the night. It was definitely getting harder to make the decision to leave.

A drunk wandered over to our table, asking for a free drink, so I gave him a dollar and told him to stay away from this table for the rest of the night. He staggered back over to the bar and left us alone after that. The dog sleeping by the foot of the bar got up and left when the drunk nearly stumbled over him.

I noticed a group of six men standing at the bar, drinking and being rowdy. One of them had a shirt on that looked kind of familiar to me. I kept telling myself, now where have I seen that shirt before? Then I noticed he was also sporting a sling on his arm, like he maybe had been shot or winged. Was it possible that this guy had been injured with a bullet crease to the shoulder by my gun and came into town earlier to see the doctor? I wasn't quite sure who these fellows were, so I whispered to Jennifer, asking her if she knew who those six men drinking together at the bar were. She said they were cowhands who worked for the Double D Bar Ranch, ten miles out of town. I decided that I was overreacting because I was carrying so much cash on me, and I was becoming a bit nervous, assuming that cowhands were outlaws, so I decided to kiss Jennifer good-bye and go back to the hotel, which was exactly what I did. I packed my gear and had it ready to leave first thing in the morning. I also cleaned up and straightened up the room. Since there was nothing more I could do about anything tonight, I would have to sleep with one eye open, half guarding my room and only half sleeping through the night, protecting my money in case someone decided to come back to my room. Actually, it was good thinking on my part because someone did try to get in through my room door during the night, and I shot right through the door, killing the intruder in self-defense again.

Now *that* really made me on the outs with Sheriff Williams because now I had two killings in Brawley, and he was not a happy law enforcement officer. He wanted to throw me in jail and use an excuse to hang me, except the hotel night clerk said someone slipped past him at the desk during the night, and he made it a point to follow the man. He witnessed the intruder going right up to my room door and trying to break in on me. There wasn't a charge the sheriff could arrest me for because I had a good credible witness.

Again, Sheriff Williams told me to get the hell out of his town before I killed anyone else. I guess I was beginning to gain my father's notorious reputation because the people of Brawley just couldn't take a fast gun as a joke. I finished packing my gear immediately right in front of the sheriff. Before Sheriff Williams left, he collected enough money off me to replace the hotel room door. Saving my hide from the Brawley jailhouse was worth paying for the damages to the hotel. When I got out onto the dark street, I noticed how the town's early risers, who were already up, began to stay clear of me like I had the plague, taking a wide path around me so as to avoid getting too close to me and my fast gun. I was beginning to feel what it was like to have people being afraid of my gun. I didn't like that feeling at all. Now I kinda know what Pa must have felt like when people were afraid of his reputation and his gun.

Chapter II

GOING BACK HOME

It was still dark when I decided to leave Brawley behind me and slip out without anyone but the early risers in town seeing me go. I thought it would give me a head start on the trail ride back, leaving Brawley in the dust and hoping all the while no one would notice I had left until at least noontime. I especially didn't want to run into the sheriff again and maybe get arrested for not leaving town fast enough to suit him.

My travel going back should be a little easier now that I didn't have two wild stallions in tow behind me. The only thing I had to worry about was getting the ranch money back safely. Now that thought began to hit me as to which was worse: towing stallions or protecting ranch money. I realized that the problem would most definitely be the money. My very life could be in danger. I checked my pistol rounds and the shells in my Winchester rifle. So far, so good; the sun was just coming up when I finally reached the beginning of the Bitter End Trail running east to Yuma. At least no stagecoaches were being robbed on my way back to the trail on the stagecoach road. Hopefully, the trip back would be a little easier. Unknown to me at the time was that if I thought for one minute the trip back would be easier, I was sorely mistaken. You see, I had forgotten about the outlaws that robbed the stagecoach and about the possibility that they may still be lurking around in the area.

I'm on the Bitter End Trail again, heading back home. Riding this narrow trail up and down the hills and gullies was enough to make a mountain goat nervous. I was no more than fifteen minutes on it when a stranger approached me from behind, catching up with me, and said, "Howdy, cowboy." When he wasn't looking, I was cautious enough to loosen the thong from my pistol.

"I'm heading for Yuma," he said. "Mind if I travel along with you for some company?"

"Suit yourself, stranger, but I would rather travel alone," I said.

"You are not a very friendly person, are you?" said the stranger.

"Actually, I'm not a very sociable person either, mister. I'm a loner."

"My name's Cullen. What's yours?"

"I'm called the Cimarron Kid. So why don't you pass me by and ride on ahead of me where I can keep you in plain sight."

"The Cimarron Kid? That sounds like a tough gunfighter tag to me," said Cullen.

"It could very well be, mister," I replied.

"Jeez! What are you nervous about, Cimarron? You hiding something or running from someone, Kid?"

"What I'm doing is none of your business. Matter of fact, if you must know, I'm just heading home to my ranch. I would like to get there as fast as I can."

"Well, if that's all you are doing, there's no reason we can't ride together. This trail gets very dark and lonely at night, and it takes seven days to get to Yuma. We can take turns building up a fire for night camp and cooking. What do you say?"

"Suit yourself, mister. But stay clear of me. I got a short temper and a fast gun. So don't do anything to rile me."

"Okay. Calm down, kid, and I'll remember that," said Cullen. "Your fast gun will also be a safety net for me too."

By the position of the sun, it must have been around noontime when I pulled up the rein and decided that my horse, Whiskey, was in need of a break and a drink at the creek that I can hear trickling in the woods off the trail. Cullen made a campfire, while I filled up our canteens and the coffeepot with water from that nearby trickling stream. I fashioned a spear from some dry branches and was able to spear a couple of brook trout from that clear and peaceful water supply. My reflexes are fast, and the fish are not in the habit of being disturbed in these woods, so they were an easy catch.

I field-dressed the fish by the stream and went back to the campfire and put on the coffee and started cooking our lunch. Cullen was surprised that I caught the fish so fast and was happy to get a decent lunch.

"How did you catch those fish, Cimarron?" questioned Cullen.

"I speared them with a switch I cut. I'm part Cherokee Indian on my pa's side of the family."

"Jeez, kid! You speared two fish in that stream that fast? You gotta have really fast reflexes to do something like that," replied Cullen.

"I do. It's the Indian bloodline," I answered. That's all I said. I was amused that Cullen swallowed hard in a nervous reaction. We both sat down by the campfire and enjoyed the tasty lunch of fish.

"Hey, Cimarron. You make a good pot of coffee too," said Cullen.

"Drink it up quick because I'm packing up and leaving soon," I replied. "Just warning you to keep up, if you don't want to get left behind."

Cullen knew that this Cimarron Kid was nobody to mess around with. The Kid was tough and very independent. Cimarron can chew up nails and spit out tacks. In fact, he was like that nasty little weed called bull nettle, with stickers all over it. If you get too close to him or brush up against him, you would have to pull the stickers out of you one at a time.

I offered Cullen another cup of coffee, and he didn't want it, so I took one last cup for myself. Dumping the rest of the pot on the campfire, I put it out and packed up Whiskey to leave. I finished swallowing down the last cup of coffee and stuck the tin cup in my saddlebags as I mounted Whiskey. To my amusement, Cullen was hustling to keep up with me. I really didn't give a shit if he got left behind. I don't trust anybody, and I like travelling alone, unless, of course, if I'm travelling with my brothers. I checked the top of my hat, and it was dusty from the trip, and I blew on it to clear the dust off it with my breath and rode away. Cullen mounted his horse and quickly caught up behind me as we rode on up the trail.

Five hours later on up the trail, it was time to give Whiskey another rest and start finding a good spot for a night camp.

"Hey, Cullen. Slide off an' cool your saddle. We're making camp here," I said.

Cullen helped me set up a dry camp for the night, and I threw on another pot of coffee. I was always a big coffee drinker, because as my Pa says, coffee stimulates the reflexes and keeps them muscles limbered and fast. Cullen was riding with me, and I had every intention of keeping my reflexes fast. The bag of coffee beans in my saddlebags was getting lighter; however, when I left home, it must have weighed about five pounds. I still had enough jerky because I was eating mostly small game and fish on the ride into Brawley, and I continued to do that on the ride back out toward Yuma.

Cullen and I took turns on night guard throughout the night hours since the Bitter End Trail had a bad reputation of being unforgiving with highwaymen and outlaws. These outlaws had no mercy when they hijacked goods by force. I woke up early in the morning to the flickering of the sunlight through the trees as the sun rose slowly above the horizon. Instead of guarding the camp, Cullen had fallen asleep and was cozy as a baby in his bedroll. I kicked him to wake his ass up with a start.

"What do you think you're doing, sleeping? You're supposed to be on guard duty for the camp."

"It's been so quiet all night I really didn't think anybody would bother us," said Cullen.

"I'm afraid I don't agree with you, Cullen. It was your turn on night guard, and that meant until morning. You should have been doing your job. Anybody could have come down on us, killed us, or robbed us. What is the matter with you? Ain't you got any brains?"

"I don't know what your problem is, Cimarron, but whenever you wake up, you are as gritty as aigs rolled in sand! So what *is* your damn problem?"

"You are my problem, cowboy. I don't intend to stay up on night guard all night, every night, when there are two of us to share that responsibility. I also don't intend to be babysitting a greenhorn on the trail. So do your proper share, or get out and let me ride alone. I told you in the beginning, I was a loner and don't need you to rile me. Let's eat quick and break camp."

Just like our first day, our second day on the Bitter End Trail was not without any problems. First thing I did was wet my face with water from my canteen to wake myself up so I could be alert for anything that comes down the trail, and come down the trail it did.

Two more drifters showed up and wanted to join us, giving me a really bad feeling about this whole situation. It wasn't to my liking at all. This quiet trail was all of a sudden getting much too crowded for me; it was like everybody was out for a Sunday horseback ride. "Where were all these drifters, with their horses packed like cowhands, coming from?" was the question in my mind. I've been on this trail a few times before, and I never saw this trail get this busy this fast. The only threats I encountered before were Mother Nature's animals.

The strangers insisted they ride along with us, and I let Cullen convince me of that because he was confident that it would be fine. This development was not sitting easy with me, and no way in hell did I like it. This also meant I would be sleeping with one eye open all the time. Now that I had three strangers riding with me, my gun was kept loaded, and the thong on my holster was always kept loose, unhooked from my gun, with my gun ready for action.

The third day was uneventful, with the exception of the three wild rabbits I shot for our supper. I couldn't help but notice that the three riders travelling with me were in awe of the speed with which I fanned my gun, not to mention that they also noticed the accuracy of my sharpshooting. Their eyes just shifted around, looking at each other. *Good,* I thought. *Looks like I made them nervous.* That was my way of giving them a silent but point-blank warning as to my skills with lead. I guess my warning was taken seriously because they figured out another way around me.

I had one eye open as Cullen came in from night watch for the camp and switched guards with the one named Pete. I sat up on my bedroll, still half asleep, when someone slipped up behind me, and I never heard them. After that, I don't know a thing that happened because that someone buffaloed me across the head with the butt of their gun, and I blacked out cold with a possible concussion. I know it was a good concussion from a very hard hit, because when I woke up with my hands and feet tied, I was seeing double and couldn't clear my head. There were some flashing lights, confusion, and I was feeling very tired. I really don't have a clue as to how many days I was out cold, stuck in what I thought was a cabin, but I remember someone kicking me in the stomach, and I vomited on the floor from the pain and nausea. After I shot the cat, I blacked out again on my empty stomach. When I woke up again, they were talking about being in a line shack.

I could hear them talking about how they took my money belt off me and split the money evenly between them. I recognized the three voices of Cullen, Pete, and Ace, the three men that were riding the Bitter End Trail with me. I did not recognize the other three voices, so they must have been at the line shack when I was brought in. They made mention of the Double D Bar Ranch, so I suspected they were the same six men I saw drinking in the bar during my last night in Brawley. Darn it. Why didn't I listen to my first own instinct when I suspected them to be outlaws? They could be the very outlaws that robbed the stage. I realized that I was in a really bad situation here and had no idea how I was going to get out of it, especially when they began to mention the stage robbery in a conversation. That's when I knew for sure they were the outlaws I was witness to. Is that why they kidnapped me, or was it a simple case of robbery?

"Hey, Ace. Why did you and Pete beat the Cimarron Kid up so bad? His eye is still swollen shut, and the bruises on his face are showing black and blue now."

"It's called uncorkin' a bronc. We took off his rough edges because we didn't want him causing us any trouble before we get rid of him. He needed to be taught a lesson as to who has the upper hand. His fast gun ain't worth a shit the way he is now, especially after he shot down John's brother in town."

I shot down somebody's brother in town? I thought. *I'm in deeper shit than I originally thought.* I tried to remember which guy it was that the sheriff said had relatives: the guy at the corral or the guy at the hotel? I was feeling confusion.

"If we are getting rid of him anyway, it seems to me to be a bit of overkill, beating him nearly to death," said Cullen.

"You going soft on us, Cullen?" said Pete. "Maybe you got just a little too friendly with him while riding the Bitter End Trail." Pete laughed. "You were only supposed to keep him busy and distracted while we robbed him."

"I told you I didn't like this plan from the very beginning. It plainly stinks," said Cullen.

"It wasn't your choice to make," said Pete. "The boss makes the decisions. Not us. You better not be backing out on this deal."

"Suppose someone looking for him finds this line shack belonging to the Double D Bar Ranch? The whole ranch will be in trouble," said Cullen.

"Shut up and quit your bellyaching, Cullen. We'll get rid of the body, and no one will find him."

"When, Pete?" said Cullen.

"When the time is right and things cool down. You got your share of the money, so shut up and quit worrying," said Pete. "When John and Luke get back, we'll do something with him."

With that last statement, I knew my time was getting short, and I needed to think of something fast. But what? I was feeling very drowsy, and sleep began to overcome me again. There is no doubt in my mind that I have a concussion. How bad it is, I really don't know.

~~~T2~~~

Ricki rang the triangle to signal that supper was ready for her family. Ty, Sundell, and Gage came wandering across the ranch from the barns and corrals. Nevada, who was working in the tack shop, washed his hands and strolled up to the porch. They all sat down to a well-prepared meal of beef and biscuits in the dining room of the remodeled, spacious ranch house. They were passing around the plates of food family style and serving themselves when TJ walked through the front door.

"Sit down, TJ, and join us for supper," said Nevada. "How is Aunt Martha doing?"

"Aunt Martha is doing fine. She already made me supper at the other ranch house. But I'll join you for coffee and dessert. Looks like Ma baked that graham cracker cake again. I can whiff it throughout the house."

"She sure did, and we are going to polish that off right after dinner," said Nevada. "Hey, TJ. How did Cimarron make out? Did he give you the money from the sale?"

"Actually, Pa, that's what I rode over here to tell you. I didn't get the sale money from him yet. I got to enter it into the books really soon so I can do the end-of-the-month report. I'm guessing he's not back yet."

"What do you mean 'he's not back yet'? He was supposed to be back three days ago. At least that's what his telegram said. I figured he was back and working the other side of the ranch with you."

"No, Pa. I thought he was working this part of the ranch with you, until Ty told me different. I'm concerned, and I thought I better ride over here and tell you. I did ride into Yuma first and send a telegram to Mr. Russell in Brawley and got an answer back right away. Cimarron left Brawley ten days ago and should have been back here three days ago. Mr. Russell checked with the hotel clerk for me to confirm it. He paid his hotel bill and left before sunup. Cimarron has disappeared. He is not in Brawley, and no one has seen him for ten days, according to the sheriff there."

"Well, hell's bells, what went wrong? Where is he?"

"Oh my god! Something went wrong! He's never been this late before. Nevada, something bad happened!" said Ricki. "I can just feel it."

"Take it easy, darlin'. We'll figure this out. He must have gotten sidetracked is all. We don't know for sure if he got sidetracked or involved with another woman. That's happened before too."

"But he was carrying a lot of money on him, Nevada. He may have been robbed, or worse!" said Ricki. "And he was travelling on that notorious Bitter End Trail!"

"Relax, darlin'. I'll take care of this. Ty, go out to the bunkhouse and tell Smokey to call in all the hands. I am having a ranch meeting at the bunkhouse in an hour."

"Sure, Pa." Ty dropped his fork on the plate and took off running to find Smokey and tell him to set up a meeting at the bunkhouse.

Chapter III

IN PURSUIT OF A
MISSING SON

Everyone from the ranch gathered around for the meeting at the bunkhouse of the Flying T2 Roughstock and Cattle Company.

"Listen up, boys. We got a problem here. The Cimarron Kid has been missing for three days, and he had a lot of ranch money on him. Smokey and I are going to backtrack his steps, and we're taking TJ, Ty, Sundell, and Gage with us. We are expecting to be gone for a couple of weeks or more, and I'm leaving Che Che Bean, as foreman, in charge of the Flying T2 Ranch. You take all your orders from Che Che Bean while Smokey and I are gone. We are leaving first thing in the morning. We're taking the Bitter End Trail into Brawley, California, the same way Cimarron went in and out. If Cimarron shows up here at the ranch in a few days, send us a telegram to Brawley, contact Jesse Russell, and let us know he came back."

"Jeez! What happened, boss?" asked Matt Jefferson.

"We haven't got a clue, Matt. He may have met with danger on the trail. That's what we are going to find out."

"Good luck, boss. Safe trails to y'all. Hope you find him safe," said Umbrella Head.

"Thank you. You boys keep this ranch going for me. We got a cattle drive to get up to Denver before the snow flies. I'm counting on you boys to get all the branding and marking done."

"We'll get 'er done, boss man," said Matt Jefferson, Nevada's black cowhand.

"Okay, Smokey and my boys, we're packing all our gear and a grubstake tonight. We are leaving at first daylight for Brawley," said Nevada.

"Sundell, tie on a pack for my horse and a bedroll. I'll run up to Ma's kitchen and gather a grubstake for us all," said TJ.

"Okay, TJ," replied Sundell.

TJ ran up to the house. "I need a grubstake for six of us, Ma. And, Ma, check in on Aunt Martha while I'm gone and tell her I went with Pa and the boys to find Cimarron. We should be back in about two weeks or so."

"Oh my gosh! I want to go with y'all."

"You can't, Ma. It's too dangerous. You got to stay here and run the ranch with Che Che Bean," said TJ. "I promise, we will all be back as soon as we can. I'll sleep in the bunkhouse tonight and leave with Pa and the boys first thing in the morning."

~~~T2~~~

The six of them headed out for Brawley, California, before the sun peeked over the horizon, announcing daylight. There was a light drizzle coming down. A little bit of wind was stirring up the landscape, moving some tumbleweeds around. Being the fall of the year, it would not be unusual for an early snowfall to surprise them. The air had a slight bite to it as they walked the horses along. When they reached the narrow path leading up to the Bitter End Trail, they entered it, and they stayed on the trail heading west toward California and the border town of Brawley.

The Nevada Kid had a lot of concerns on his mind, and as he travelled, he was very quiet, just thinking, *What could have happened to Cimarron? Was it likely that someone could have outgunned him? My kid is a sharpshooter and a very fast gun, faster than I ever was on the draw. It would be hard to believe someone was faster on the draw than Cimarron, unless, for some reason, he let his guard down. What will I do? How will I react in front of the rest of my sons should I find his body on the trail? How will I explain it all to Ricki, his mother?*

"Nevada. You're pushing us too hard. We need to stop and give the horses a rest. It would be a good time for some lunch," replied Smokey, interrupting Nevada's concentration.

"Yeah, Pa. I'm hungry," replied Gage.

"You're always hungry, Gage," answered Nevada.

"That young pup needs his nourishment, Pa. He is a growing boy," laughed TJ, the oldest of the boys.

"All right. We'll stop in this clearing just ahead. Sundell, take care of the horses. Ty and Gage, make a campfire. TJ, get the grub out," ordered Nevada.

"I'll put the coffee on, Nevada," said Smokey. Smokey noticed that Nevada checked the rounds in his pistol and his rifle. Nevada wasn't taking any chances. Smokey figured he better do the same.

"I'm gonna ride out in a few minutes and scout the trail ahead of us for a way. I should be right back, Smokey." He checked the cinch on his horse and tightened the strap.

"Okay, Nevada," replied Smokey. "Ain't you gonna eat nothin'?"

"When I get back," said Nevada.

"C'mon, Ty and Gage. Hustle up with that firewood, you boys. Jeez. You two are so slow that if you ever lay down by a river to get yourselves a drink, the weeds would grow over both of you," mimicked Smokey.

"We're trying, Smokey! There ain't much wood around here," said Ty.

"Yeah, and besides, it's all wet from the drizzle," said Gage.

"Well, the drizzle stopped, so pull the dry stuff from underneath the brush," replied Smokey. "Watch out for snakes too."

"Hey, Smokey. You coming down hard on my boys again?" laughed Nevada.

"Yeah. They need it. Remember how green you were when I first met you, Nevada? How about Blackie, the first outlaw that needed killing by your gun, and what did you do after? You shot the cat behind the rocks. Thought I didn't know you lost your whole supper, didn't you?" Smokey laughed. "I rode a lot of trails with you, pard, and I raised you up on those trails too. You ain't turned out to be too bad either."

"Yeah, well, their mother is protective of them. Nothing I can do about that."

"Just let them ride trail with us for a while. I'll toughen them up like I did you, the way they should be. I toughened up Cimarron too, didn't I?"

"No, you didn't, Smokey. Cimarron was born that tough. I've even seen you back down from him on more than one occasion."

"All right. So you got me on that one," laughed Smokey.

"Okay. I'll be right back," said Nevada. He mounted Tacco and rode out.

Nevada moved on up the trail, scouting for tracks or any kind of sign he could find that would show him a trace of Cimarron having travelled through the area. Nevada's tracking skills were so good he could track a bear through running water. He found nothing. There were also no signs of anyone travelling on the trail either. A little farther up the trail, he found an old campfire where a single person had camped for the night. The campfire looked to be about two weeks old or more. There is a possibility Cimarron camped here on his way across the trail to California. Nevada was quite sure Cimarron did not get this far up the Bitter End Trail on his way back from Brawley. He headed back to the camp for some lunch with the boys.

"Well, Nevada, did you find anything?" inquired Smokey.

"Not a thing, Smokey," Nevada answered. "If he was travelling back on this trail, he didn't get this far yet. I'll have to keep a close eye out as we move farther on."

Smokey handed Nevada a tin plate full of food. He accepted it without a word. They ate a quick meal of bacon and beans.

"Hey, TJ. What's that you just pulled out of the sack?" asked Nevada.

"Oh. It's graham cracker cake, Pa. I brought the leftovers with us," he said.

"Well, pass it around, boy," said Nevada. "You ain't keeping that to yourself. You gotta share it," Nevada laughed.

"Nevada. That wife of yours sure can bake really good," replied Smokey.

"She sure can," answered Nevada. "She has to do a lot of baking to keep all these boys in snacks."

"Who do you think you're kidding, Pa? She bakes for your sweet tooth, and ya know it," said Ty. Nevada just laughed.

"All right, let's break camp and keep moving," said Nevada. "The faster we find Cimarron, the better I'll feel. We don't know if his being missing is life threatening or not. Let's go, boys. Hustle up."

They moved ahead quickly, travelling at a steady pace while watching the Bitter End Trail for any signs of struggle or any clues that may indicate foul play. As it got later into the evening, they decided to set up camp under the falling darkness. The chill in the air necessitated a campfire and a pot of coffee to take the shivers out of their bones. The Bitter End Trail was pitch-dark and lonely at night, and no sounds could be heard, except for those of Mother Nature. The dark silence was almost like being out in space or in another dimension of time. An occasional rustle could be heard in the thickness of the underbrush or in the trees. The softness of the rustle would startle one of them out of a sound sleep, only to have them roll over and return to sleep again. A fast breakfast in the morning, and they were moving on along the trail again.

They travelled the Bitter End Trail for a week now, and there were no telltale signs of anything they could find relating to Cimarron. Not even a dead body or sign of a struggle, no dead animals, not a single empty cartridge from a gun—nothing. At lunchtime, Nevada scouted ahead again. He came back at a gallop.

"Hey, Smokey, boys. The Bitter End Trail ends just up ahead. It comes out into a clearing, and there is a stagecoach road headed for the town of Brawley. There's a sign pointing southwest that says Brawley Fifteen Miles. We don't have a choice. We're heading on into Brawley. I got questions I want answered," said Nevada.

"Nevada, we can use a new grubstake too," said Smokey. "These boys of yours just about ate up everything we got!"

"Pa, I'm tired of riding," said Gage. "I'm saddle sore. I could eat a good, juicy rare steak too."

"I know it's been a long week, boys. We'll get rooms at the hotel, and I'll see if I can get some straight answers from anybody in town on the whereabouts of Cimarron. Let's go, boys. We'll head straight on into town."

Chapter IV

BRAWLEY, CALIFORNIA

Brawley was a forlorn-looking town, and yet it was brimming with activity and excitement. The town was still building up to become a decent place for folks to live. On the way into town, Smokey and the Lacey family passed a one-room schoolhouse that was in the process of being built. A stack of lumber lay beside it, and the carpenters were pulling boards from the pile. You could hear hammering and sawing, and one workman was plying an ax. The border town was gradually transforming from a lawless border town into a thriving place to live. Some of the building structures were still false-fronted, but they were painted in bright colors so as to give the town a look of urban greatness and to inspire new settlers to come in to stay and make a home in California.

They walked the horses up the main street, which still had a mud puddle here and there, left from a previous rainstorm. They passed a boot maker's shop, a barbershop, a hotel, a doctor's office, a bank, a general store, two saloons, a bawdy house, a telegraph office, and a butcher shop. These townsmen were providing goods and services to the population in the area. Most of the people living in the area around the town were ranchers grazing their cattle on the limitless grasslands, and Nevada looked upon these ranchers as prospective clients who will buy stock from his ranch. However, this town of Brawley was not without drama because it had its share of prostitutes, scalawags, shysters, and desperadoes. As they walked their horses down the main street, they were getting stared at by the folks, and they felt as unwelcome as a tax collector or even as a polecat at a picnic.

The first thing they did was to stop by the sheriff's office and introduce themselves. Nevada did not want to take any chances because of the townsfolk staring up at the six strangers riding into town together as if they were some kind of outlaw threat. Their entrance into town caused a lot of suspicion as to who they were and what they were up to. Nevada and Smokey dismounted and tethered their horses to the rail as the sheriff came out of his office and looked them all over.

"Good day, sheriff. My name's Tom Lacey. This here is my foreman, Smokey Embers, and the four boys there are my sons, TJ, Ty, Sundell, and Gage." Nevada offered his hand, and the sheriff took it reluctantly for the handshake.

"Wow, that's a powerful, strong handshake, Mr. Lacey. I almost figured it was you. I finally get to meet the Nevada Kid himself in person. The picture on my Wanted poster some years back didn't do you any justice. I was looking out the window and noticed the Flying T2 Brand on all those horses as you boys rode up. I saw that brand about ten days ago on the Cimarron Kid's horse. What brings all of you boys into my town?"

"Just that, sheriff. The Cimarron Kid. My son is missing. He never arrived home from Brawley. I'm out looking for him, and I got a lot of questions to ask of this here town." The four young cowboys dismounted.

"What do you want to know, Nevada? I'm Sheriff Williams, and he ain't in my jail, although he should be."

"Why do you say he should be in your jail, sheriff?"

"He shot and killed two men while he was here in town, and I better not see his face around here again. I told him to get out of town as soon as his business was done."

The four young cowboys looked at each other silently, questioning the statement by the sheriff.

"When did he leave town, if he did leave this here town?"

"He left before dawn ten days ago. I haven't seen him since. In fact, Jesse Russell and I both answered a telegram from your son, TJ. He left town, and he is not here. As I understand it, he took the Bitter End Trail back home."

"We just came from the Bitter End Trail, sheriff. There is no sign that he was ever coming back through there. What happened in this town while he was here? I want to know everything that went on. So what else can you tell me, especially about these shootings you mentioned?"

"Well, he shot and killed Dave Spence in self-defense down at the corral. I was a witness to that one. It seems Dave was messing with the horses Cimarron brought in for the Pinion Pine Ranch. They got into an argument over the treatment of the horses, and Dave pulled a fast draw. Cimarron outdrew Dave and killed him point-blank. I told Cimarron I wanted him out of town in twenty-four hours as soon as his business was done. I saw the whole thing go down, and it *was* self-defense. Then the night before he left town, his room was ransacked. He filled out a report on it and signed the complaint. Nothing was stolen, but he gave me a full report and signed it just for the record. You're welcome to see the report."

"Yes. I want to see that report, sheriff."

Sheriff Williams invited them into his office and showed them the report. Nevada passed the report around to the others. The signature on the report was definitely written by Cimarron's hand. "So you found nothing? Nothing was missing, and all you found was a mess?"

"That is correct. His money belt was not stolen because, as he said, he had it on him."

"So what did he do after he filed the report?" questioned Nevada.

"Well, I thought he went back to the Cattle Call Hotel. But someone else told me they saw him at the saloon with Jennifer that same night."

"Seeing Cimarron with a girl makes a lot more sense as to his personality. Who is this Jennifer?" questioned Nevada.

"She's one of the girls that work at the Branding Iron Saloon & Dance Hall. He was seen with her a few times while he was here in town," replied Sheriff Williams. "We suspected he was hanging out with her in the evenings."

"Anything else you think I need to know, sheriff?" asked Nevada.

"Sure is, Nevada. That kid of yours shot and killed the second man trying to break into his room early in the morning before he left town. He paid for the damages though. I wanted to arrest his ass for the second killing and hang him, but he was lucky the night clerk was a witness to someone trying to break in and kill Cimarron. So again, it was self-defense. There isn't another thing I can tell you, Nevada. That's all I know. But I will add this. I hear you got a good reputation with a gun. While you and your boys are here in my town, I want your guns left here in my office. I won't tolerate any more killings from this roughneck family of yours, Nevada. You hear me, Kid? I mean what I say. Any one of you boys that gets his bad ass in trouble, in my town, goes straight to jail. You got that?"

"Sure do, sheriff. Okay, boys. Everybody, unload the hardware and leave it here. I don't want any more trouble with this town or Sheriff Williams," said Nevada.

"But, Nevada—," interrupted Smokey.

"Do it, Smokey. You heard Sheriff Williams," replied Nevada.

"Damn," replied Smokey. "I feel naked without my gun!" They all passed their guns to the sheriff, who was happy to collect them.

"Thanks, sheriff. We will be checking into the hotel for a couple of days, and you'll probably see us around for a while. Let's go, boys. We'll get our rooms and wash up. Where's a good place to eat, sheriff?

"Go to Zanelli's Café. It's the best food in town, and it's down near the Branding Iron Saloon."

"Thanks, sheriff."

They left the sheriff's office and untethered their horses, walking them down the street toward the Cattle Call Hotel. They tied the horses to the rail in front of the hotel, and they had to shoo the chickens away on the boardwalk before they could get in through the door and up to the desk.

"Good day, gentlemen," said the clerk at the desk. He was a thin, bony man with glasses. "What can I do for you?"

"I want three rooms with two beds in each one," said Nevada. "And we are gonna need plenty of hot water to wash off the trail dust."

"Yes, sir. Right away, sir. Rooms 4, 5, and 6. Here are your keys, sir. Hey, Charlie. Three bathtubs and hot water for rooms 4, 5, and 6. When will you pay for it, sir? On a tab or up front?" The clerk turned the register book and looked at the names.

"Make a bill out to the Flying T2 Ranch. I'll pay for the three rooms and run a tab for them. My name's the Nevada Kid. These boys are my four sons. I'll pay you before we leave."

"Okay, sir, but I'll have to charge for the hot water. I'll put it on your tab. My goodness! The Nevada Kid. I've heard of you, sir. Oh my gosh!"

Nevada boldly turned the register book back around and found the entry where Cimarron signed himself in and out, making a note of it in his mind. The scared clerk watched him but did not stop him from checking the names. "That's not allowed, sir," said the clerk gently. Nevada just ignored him with a hard stare. The clerk backed off from the stare.

Nevada turned and glanced at Smokey, and Smokey was grinning and silently giggling. This new experience also seemed to be amusing to the Lacey boys that everyone in town was nervous around their father, the famous gunfighter from the Younger Brothers Gang. Everybody they encountered seemed to know Nevada's reputation and who he was. Nevada and Smokey took room 4. TJ and Ty took room 5, across the hall. Sundell and Gage took room 6.

When they finished bathing and freshening up, they all met in the hall, then headed downstairs to find Zanelli's Café and get some supper. But before they left the hotel, Nevada went up to the desk clerk.

"What's that room number again that my son, Cimarron, stayed in while he was here?" he asked.

"It was room 10, Mr. Nevada," said the nervous clerk.

"When I come back later on, will you show me that room? I have some questions to ask you also."

"Yes, sir. I will do that," said the obviously nervous clerk.

Nevada left the desk. "Let's go get something to eat, boys," he said.

They crossed the street from the hotel and strolled down the boardwalk, past a brothel with a couple of ladies on the balcony and a couple standing in the doorway downstairs. The girls called to the boys, waving to them and luring them to come on in for some fun.

"Come on in, you cowboys. Wow, six of you! Did a trail drive just come in? Boy, y'all are handsome, good-looking young men too," said one of the girls. "Yessiree. A couple of *really* young ones."

"We got a few tricks to show you boys," said another girl. "C'mon in. Wow! I never saw so many good-lookin' men and young cowboys all in one group. We hit the jackpot, girls."

"Hey, Pa," said Gage.

"Don't even think about it," said Nevada. "You're too young."

"But, Pa, I was only gonna ask you if they're what I think they are."

Nevada gave Gage a hard look. Smokey couldn't contain his laughter. *Gage was a greenhorn ranch kid, all right,* thought Smokey. *The extent of Gage's travels included circling around a campfire in cow camp, looking for the handle on the coffee pot.*

"Hey, Gage. If you really want to please the ladies, you got to age a little bit more and grow your fuse just a little bit longer," laughed Smokey.

"Smokey!" said Nevada. "That's enough."

"Now who did you say was being overprotective of the boys, Nevada? Did I hear you say it was *you* or Ricki?" laughed Smokey.

"Shut up, Smokey. It ain't funny."

"Maybe you should get the boys off that ranch a little more often. If they're old enough to work, they are old enough to play."

"Cut it out, Smokey. I said it ain't funny."

"Well, at least we know Cimarron doesn't let any grass grow under his feet when it comes to women and travelling."

"Stop heckling me. You're making me mad. We'll find out what kind of trouble *he* got himself into right after we get us a bite to eat," replied Nevada.

They came up to Zanelli's Café and went inside.

"There's a table for six in that far corner," said a worker in the café. "What are you boys drinking?"

"Bring six beers," belted out Smokey. The server walked away to the kitchen.

Nevada looked in question at Smokey. "Six beers?"

"It's about time you start treating these boys like the young men they are, Nevada. Besides, Ricki will never know they're drinking if she ain't here."

Nevada turned to his sons. "Did you boys want beer?" asked Nevada.

"Sure we do, Pa," answered TJ. "I've been drinking beer since college, and I just never told you. Besides, Ty, Sundell, and Gage have been drinking up my supply over at my ranch house. Aunt Martha just kept it quiet and never told you. I love Aunt Martha. She's so cool."

"Is there anything else I need to know about you boys that I don't already know?" questioned Nevada.

"Well, only that Gage has a girlfriend in Yuma, and she is fifteen, and they kiss a lot, and Cimarron has been teasing him about what else he could do," said Sundell.

"Cimarron what!" said Nevada.

"Shut up, Sundell. Pa doesn't need to know all that," said Gage.

"You ain't got enough ranch chores to do, boy?" questioned Nevada.

Smokey, at this point, was laughing hysterically.

"When I get y'all back home, we are gonna have some serious long talks about such things," replied Nevada.

"Tell them, Nevada. Tell them all of what you know about such things," Smokey laughed. Nevada just furrowed his brows, giving Smokey a stern look.

"You're not helping me any, Smokey."

"Yessiree. The Lacey boys are growing up fast into men, Nevada," laughed Smokey.

"You don't need to have that talk, Pa. We already know about everything," explained Ty. "It ain't any different than breeding cattle and roughstock or taking care of cattle during calving season. The breeding charts are all hanging on the walls in the bunkhouse. We've been studying them."

"Shit," said Nevada. "I should have known. You boys have been spending a lot of time in that bunkhouse with the cowhands?"

"Hell, yeah," said Ty. "Among other things, we've been learning how to play cards too!"

Smokey just kept on giggling. "Did you pick up on that, Nevada? He said 'among other things,'" laughed Smokey. "Ha ha ha!"

The server came back to the table and passed the beers around. "So, boys, what are you eating for lunch today?"

"I want a steak, Pa," said Gage. "Done rare."

"How is that son-of-a-gun stew?" asked Nevada.

"It's excellent. It was made fresh this morning for the lunch crowd."

"Is that okay with everybody else?" said Nevada.

"Yeah, Pa," the group agreed.

"Okay. One steak for Gage here, done rare, and bring five bowls of that son-of-a-gun stew, with some biscuits and gravy. If you have any apple pie, bring that for dessert with coffee."

"You got it, boys. I'll be right back," said the server. Three servers were carrying all the food dishes to the table when the waitress came back. They helped her place the order on the table. The starving boys began digging in.

"How's that steak, Gage?" asked Nevada.

"It's done perfectly, Pa. Just the way I like it."

"Okay. Here's the plan. After we eat, we will go over to the saloon and find that girl, Jennifer. We'll see if we can get some answers out of her. We will also check the telegraph office and talk to the clerk. If we don't get any answers there, we will ride out to the Pinion Pine Ranch."

Chapter V

THE BRANDING IRON SALOON & DANCE HALL

They entered the Branding Iron Saloon & Dance Hall through the batwing doors to the sound of a player piano and the strong scent of smoke and liquor hitting them square in the face. The floor was covered with a combination of sawdust and peanut shells, which made the dance hall slippery enough and easy to slide boots across on a two-step dance sequence. Around the shuffleboard game table, some of its wax fell onto the dance floor and actually made that area of the floor extremely slippery. This was the area on the dance floor where the cowboys loved to spin out with the girls really fast because it was a slick spot under their worn-out boots.

A saloon girl was belting out "Old Joe Clark" while standing next to the piano, and the dancers were hooting and howling when they spun out fast by the shuffleboard game table. The saloon was very noisy and gay.

"Wow! This place is neat," replied Gage. "Look at that naked picture over the bar!" His brothers giggled.

Nevada didn't answer him this time, having seen many of the same kinds of portraits in his travels around with the Younger Brothers Gang. The jezebel pictures in these frontier bars were a major entertaining experience in themselves for cowhands to witness.

Nevada pointed to an empty round table with about five empty chairs, and his boys walked over to it and sat down. TJ pulled a sixth chair from a side table and sat down with the others. Smokey and Nevada went up to the bar and ordered a full round of beers for the table. The bartender nodded his head and said he would bring them right over.

"I need some information. I'm looking for a girl named Jennifer. Does she work here?" asked Nevada.

"Yeah. She is the girl singing by the piano," said the bartender.

"I'd like to buy her whatever she drinks. Can you get it for her and send her over to my table?"

"Sure, mister. That will be another dollar." Nevada tossed the money on the bar, and he and Smokey went over to the table to sit down with his boys. The bartender brought a tray of full beer mugs over. He set them on the table one at a time, and the boys passed them around the table.

About five minutes later, Jennifer came over with her drink in her hand, and TJ, being a cultured gentleman, stood up and offered her his chair.

"Thank you. You are a real gentlemen, cowboy."

TJ tipped his hat to her. "Ma'am," he said.

"Who do I thank for this drink, boys?"

Smokey pointed to Nevada.

"Thank you, sir. What is your name? Do I know you? You have a very familiar face."

"My name is Tom Lacey. I'm called the Nevada Kid. I'm from Yuma, Arizona, ma'am. In fact, we are all the Lacey family from Yuma."

"Now I know who you look like. You look like the Cimarron Kid. You could pass for brothers," said Jennifer.

"Actually, ma'am, I'm his father. These four boys are his brothers. That's TJ. He's Ty. That's Sundell, and that young pup staring at that picture over the bar is Gage. This fellow sitting on my right is my foreman, Smokey."

"Well, if you are all here, where is Cimarron?"

"That is what we came here to ask you, ma'am. You see, he never got home from Brawley, ma'am. We thought you might know something about his whereabouts."

"Oh my gosh, no. I love that cowboy. He is *so good* I, uh, well, actually, I just love that guy. He was always such a, uh, *gentleman*," she said as she looked over at young Gage.

"Now that we all understand how good you think he is, when did you last see him, ma'am?" inquired Nevada.

"Well, let's see. It was late, the night before he left for home. Yes. He came into the saloon, and I ran right up to him, and we kissed." Gage grinned wide and looked around at the others when he heard that. "Then we went to a table and sat down. In fact, it was this very table we are at now. I wanted him to stay the night, but he said no. He was leaving before sunup and heading for home. It was about ten o'clock when he left, because he looked at his watch and told me the time."

"Did anything else happen between the time he walked in here and the time he left here?"

"No. Well, yes. He asked me who the six men were that were standing at the bar, drinking. He was looking hard at the man with the sling on his arm. It seems he recognized the shirt the man was wearing, or at least he thought he did. He thought it was one of the outlaws he wounded when he chased them away from the stagecoach."

"He chased outlaws away from a stagecoach?"

"Yes. When he came out of the Bitter End Trail, the local stage was being robbed. He chased after the outlaws, shooting his rifle, and sent them fleeing. But they got away with the mail and the payroll. He said he wounded one of them. He tied his horses on the back of the stagecoach and drove the stage for the rest of the way into town. The stagecoach driver and shotgun guard were dead. Cimarron put them inside the stage."

"So then who were the six men at the bar?" asked Nevada.

"Oh. They were just the ranch hands from the Double D Bar Ranch. I guess Cimarron mistook them for the outlaws."

"What were their names, Jennifer? Do you know?"

"John Spence, the foreman, Pete, Cullen, Ace, Jay, and Luke."

"John Spence? Any relation to Dave Spence, the one Cimarron shot at the corral?"

"Why, yes. Matter of fact, they were brothers!"

Nevada looked at Smokey, and their eyes exchanged thoughts. "It looks like a visit is in order to the Double D Bar Ranch," said Nevada.

"It sure as hell does, Nevada," replied Smokey.

"So who was this other guy he shot at the hotel, Jennifer? Do you know?"

"No, sir. I only know that he also worked for the Double D Bar Ranch outfit. But I don't know his name."

"Thanks, Jennifer. You can go back to work. I have no more questions for you."

"It was nice meeting all of Cimarron's family. I hope you find him safe. Good lord, he was so good." She strolled away to the bar.

Nevada let out a heavy breath, shaking his head, while Smokey just giggled.

"Reminds me of some good ol' times, Nevada! Cimarron's a chip off the old block."

"Enough of that, Smokey," replied Nevada. "Don't go telling these boys tales out of school."

Too late, thought Smokey. *They already know about your wild streak.*

"Okay, boys. Here's the plan. Ty and Gage, go over to the telegraph office and question the clerk who sent out that telegram. Find out if anyone else knew what was in Cimarron's message besides the clerk. The rest of us will split up. Smokey and I will visit the Double D Bar Ranch, and Sundell and TJ will go over to the Pinion Pine Ranch. Ask lots of questions and find out everything you can as to when Cimarron was last seen. When you are done, we will all meet back here at this saloon and compare notes."

Chapter VI

THE INTERROGATIONS BEGIN

After lunch, Ty and Gage headed over to the telegraph office. Brawley Telegraph Office was painted across its facade in erratic black lettering. On each side of the door was a window in need of a good washing because, as they peeked in, they could barely see through the thick coating of dust sticking to it from the dusty front street. As they entered inside the small shop, they were assaulted with the smell of dust in the air, causing Gage to sneeze. The leisure sound of the telegraph key was tick, tick, ticking as their eyes became accustomed to the dimness in the little room. They were drawn inevitably toward the desk at the back end of the room, where the telegraph was singing away, and the clerk was just finishing up, writing the message down. Their spurs jingled, and their boots clumped as they walked across the rough wood flooring and up to the desk. Customers that chewed tobacco used the spittoon sitting on the floor in front of the desk. Evidence showed some of them missed as often as they scored.

"Can I help you, cowboys?" said the telegraph clerk as he turned the newly written message upside down on the desk so they couldn't read it.

"Yes, sir," said Ty. "I'm Ty Lacey, and this here is my brother, Gage. We are looking for some information that you may be able to give us some answers on. Our brother, Cimarron, was in here about two weeks ago, and he sent out a telegram to our ranch, the Flying T2 Roughstock and Cattle Company."

"I remember that fellow—yes, I do," said the clerk, "and the name of that spread. I can't tell you what was in that message though. It's private mail and against the law to discuss any messages I send out."

"We know that, sir. What we are interested in is if anyone else was in this shop at the time the message was dictated to you or when that message was sent out."

"Are you accusing me of telling that message to someone else? If you are, you two cowboys can walk right out that door now. I would never intentionally do that with a message. Don't you accuse me of it either!"

"We are not accusing you of anything, sir. We are just asking if anyone else was around when our brother's message went out on the wire," said Gage.

"Well, how would I know?" said the clerk. "There are always loungers sitting out front of my shop and in the habit of poking their noses into my business. I chase them away all the time. I even complained to the sheriff about it."

"Please, sir. It's important to us. Try and think back to that one day when Cimarron sent that message out. Was there anybody in hearing distance when Cimarron dictated that message to you?" said Ty.

"Yes, sir. Please try and remember if anyone was lounging outside your shop or if anyone walked into the shop to send a telegram out or pick one up at the same time Cimarron was in here," said Gage.

"Yes," said the clerk. "I do remember now. There was Jake, the old town drunk, out cold on the bench out front. But that was not all. Ace walked in here to pick up a telegram for Dan Donaldson. In fact, one of Dan's hands should be coming in again this afternoon to pick up this telegram that I just wrote down for Dan Donaldson. Every so often, Dan gets telegrams on stock sales and rates. Ace was here that day. He was standing in line right behind your brother, looking curiously down at your brother's low hanging gun. I didn't remember right off because your brother towered over Ace, and I really couldn't see him too good standing behind Cimarron, except for his head looking down at the gun. Then Cimarron turned and left the shop ahead of Ace. Ace's gaze followed your brother all the way out of the door."

"So who is this Ace?" replied Ty.

"He works for the Double D Bar Ranch. One of Dan Donaldson's cowhands. Ace didn't stay long. He picked up the telegram and left in a hurry. Oftentimes, he will stop at the saloon and stay in town awhile. But this time, I noticed he did a flying mount and headed straight back to the Double D without any hesitation. That's about all I can tell you boys."

"We want to thank you very much, sir, for your cooperation," said Ty.

"Henry. My name is Henry. Sorry, I can't do no more for you boys."

"You did plenty for us, Henry. Thanks again," said Ty.

"Well, what do we do now, Ty?" asked Gage.

"We'll hang around town and check out some of the shops. I need to find a new pair of boots or a boot maker who can repair the ones I have. By that time, Pa and the others should be back at our meeting point," replied Ty.

They stopped at the boot maker's shop and were in luck. While they waited, the boot maker repaired the hole in the sole of Ty's boot. Leaving there, they headed into the general store next door.

The clerk approached them as they looked around at the general merchandise. "Anything I can help you boys with?"

"Actually, sir. We are looking for a little information on our brother, Cimarron. Did a tall cowboy come in here about two weeks ago to buy any supplies for his trip back to Yuma?"

"Yes. I remember that cowboy. He brought horses to Jesse Russell. Who wouldn't remember that boy? Everybody in town was talking about that boy. He shot and killed two men in this town. He was a pretty fast gunman, even though it was all in self-defense."

"That's him," said Gage. "What exactly did he buy? Do you remember?"

"Let's see now. It was beef jerky, sugar, some flour, a piece of cheesecloth, bullets—that's it. No. I sold him some loose-leaf chewing tobacco. Yes. It was Bull Durham brand. He said he had enough coffee to get back home."

"Did you see him leave town? If so, what time?" said Ty.

"No. I heard he left before sunrise in the morning. I only know because the sheriff stopped in here, inquiring about him, and mentioned that Cimarron, that fast-gun polecat, left town early. I did not see him leave town."

"Okay. Thank you, mister," said Ty.

"You are welcome, son."

"Let's head back to the meeting point and wait for the others, Gage," said Ty.

CHAPTER VII

THE PINION PINE RANCH

TJ and Sundell walked their horses up the long dirt road leading to the Pinion Pine Ranch. Pinion Pine was not as big a spread as the one they grew up on, but it was a prominent, well-laid-out spread just the same. There were cows and bulls on its grazing lands and a large corral of good-looking horses on the road leading up to the ranch house. The ranch house itself had a nice veranda that wrapped around on three sides and a backyard view of the mountains behind it. Being the fall of the year, the mountain peaks were already capped with the beauty of its first snowfall. Trees and shrubs at the lower elevations were showing off the splendor of Mother Nature's fall colors.

As they rode up to the porch of the ranch house, someone was calling to them as he walked across the yard from the corral on the left side of the house.

"Hey there, fellows. I'm over here. What can I do for you boys? Hi. I'm Jesse Russell, the owner of this here spread." Jesse walked up to their horses. "You cowboys looking for work? I got a trail drive coming up in a few weeks. I can use a few new hands."

"No, sir," said TJ. "Actually, we are looking for some answers to a few questions, Mr. Russell. My name is TJ Lacey, and this here is my brother, Sundell."

"Well, c'mon down, boys. Tie your horses to the rail there. That name sounds awfully familiar. Any relation to Cimarron Lacey?"

The boys dismounted. "Yes, sir," said Sundell. "He's our brother, and we are looking for him. He never came home from Brawley after delivering some roughstock to you."

"Are you serious? He still never came home as yet, TJ? You are the one that sent me a telegram, inquiring about him a week ago."

"Yes, sir. We still haven't found him, and we are worried."

"Well, I'd be worried too. He was here two weeks ago."

"Yes, sir," said TJ.

Just then, a horse with a rider came flying up the dirt road toward the ranch house, and it looked out of control. Sundell ran up to the horse and grabbed its halter and reins to stop it and hold it in place. Just as he did that, the rider fell off the horse smack into TJ's arms. TJ's arms cushioned the fall as he lost his balance and fell backward on his butt and then fell flat out on his back. TJ knew only one thing: there was this beautiful-looking girl sitting smack dab in the center of his lap. His butt hurt from the hard fall, and he was lying flat on his back, looking up at her with shock on his face. She turned around and looked down at him, just as shocked because she knew damn well it was definitely not TJ's saddle horn that was growing rock hard underneath her butt.

"Oh my gosh! I am so sorry. I hope you didn't get hurt, mister. Indeed, I'm so sorry."

"Yes, ma'am" was all TJ could think of saying.

"Janice, just what the *hell* do you think you are doing? I told you a hundred times not to race that stallion. You can't use him for barrel racing. He's too wild, and you can't control him. When will you ever listen to me? Jeez. TJ, I'm so sorry, my daughter has made a fool of herself again. She just can't take my orders seriously."

"That's okay, Jesse," replied Sundell. "My brother, TJ, is used to being jumped on and thrown down in the dirt. Cimarron does it to him all the time."

"Cimarron?" said Janice. "You know Cimarron?"

"Cimarron is our brother," said Sundell. "I'm Sundell, the cleanest one of all five of us brothers. That dirty, dusty mess in the road you are now sitting on is our oldest brother, TJ. He is supposed to be the lawyer in our family, but right now, he doesn't look like much of anything!"

"Shut up, Sundell. You aren't any help, and hold onto that stallion so he doesn't bolt again and step on us."

Sundell pulled the rein, leading the horse away from the two folks on the ground. James, the foreman, came running up to Sundell and took the horse's lead.

"Put him up in the corral, James," said Jesse. "Janice, you want to get off that man so he can get up out of the dirt."

"No," said Janice. "I just thought I would sit here for a while and catch my breath! Of course, I want to get up off him, Pa," she said, with a saucy attitude.

"I'll help you, Janice," said Sundell. He offered her his hand and pulled her up. He had a sinister grin on his face and a dirty laugh as he looked back at TJ lying there in the dirt. He walked Janice to the veranda. "Did you get any dirt on you, ma'am?" he asked.

"No," she replied. "But what about TJ?"

"Oh, he's fine," said Sundell. "He is used to being dirty."

TJ was secretly pissed off as he got himself back up on his feet and followed them up to the veranda while brushing the dirt off his clothes. *Leave it to one of my younger brothers to put me down and take over charming the girl,* he thought.

"Janice," said Jesse. "Bring my bottle of brandy out here and some glasses. These boys need a drink. And make them some sandwiches or something to snack on. I'm sure they are hungry. So what happened to Cimarron? Did you boys check in town for him?"

"Well, our brothers, Ty and Gage, are checking around town. Pa and Smokey are heading out to the Double D Bar Ranch. It seems Cimarron shot and killed Dave Spence in self-defense in town over an argument concerning the stallions he was bringing you. Sheriff Williams said Dave was abusing one of the stallions, and Cimarron caught him at it and stopped him. It wound up in a gunfight at the corral, and Dave lost."

"Wow! Was it self-defense?" asked Jesse.

"Yes. Sheriff Williams said he saw Dave draw first, and Cimarron beat him to the draw."

"Dave Spence has a brother, John, who is foreman of the Double D Bar Ranch. John has a nasty temper and won't sit still for anyone shooting and killing his brother. Maybe John went after Cimarron. He's the vengeful type. You never can tell. I hope that's not the case," said Jesse.

"Yes, sir. We heard about Dave's brother, John Spence, the foreman of the Double D Bar Ranch. I think we all thought about the possibility of John's getting revenge on Cimarron," said TJ.

"You better be careful with those Double D boys," said Jesse. "They are gun-happy roughnecks that cause a lot of trouble in this area. They drink, shoot off their guns, and play practical jokes."

Janice brought out some sandwiches and brandy, setting them down on the table near the porch swing. She noticed how very handsome these two brothers were. In fact, there was a family resemblance to Cimarron that was unmistakably there. However, she noticed one difference: neither brother was wearing the beautiful silver arrowhead and chain that stood out so pronounced on Cimarron's chest.

"You know, Jesse," said TJ, "if you are looking for a really good barrel racing horse for Janice, we have some superb racing stock on our ranch. Gage and Ty have been training some beauties for the rodeo circuit down in Smithville. I'm sure they can pull out a good one for Janice."

"Would you like that, Janice?" replied Jesse.

"I would love it, Pa," said Janice.

"Okay. When you boys get back home, do that for me. Telegram me when the horse is ready. Maybe Janice and I can take a trip to your ranch to pick it up. Your pa can show us around the ranch too."

"That sounds like a great plan, Jesse. We'll do that," said Sundell.

"You know, boys," said Jesse, "I have a good bunch of ranch hands if you need a search party to help look for Cimarron. My boys are available to you for the asking. We would be glad to do all we can to find your brother."

"Thank you very much, Jesse. We will keep you and the boys in mind should we need more help," said Sundell.

"Jesse, can you give me any information on Cimarron's visit here at your ranch?" replied TJ.

"No, son. He came here and delivered the stallions and cinches, and I paid him in cash. He put the money in his leather money belt and the receipt in his pocket. He left and came back early evening and had dinner with us that night."

"That's right," said Janice. "We sat on the porch swing, and he picked up our guitar and sang some songs for me. It was around ten in the evening when he put down the guitar and left, because I heard the clock chime inside the house. That's the last we saw of him."

"I can see there is no point in hanging around here, Sundell. We best be getting back to the meeting point to see what the others may have found out. Thank you for the brandy and lunch, Jesse. And, Janice, thank you very much also," said TJ as he stood up to leave. "Let's go, Sundell."

"I'll tell you what, boys," said Jesse. "Why don't y'all come back for dinner tonight? I'd like to see your father again. It's been quite some time."

"That would be a lot of cooking, Jesse. There are six of us. It would be quite a bit of work for Janice to handle," replied TJ.

What a thoughtful and considerate guy this TJ is, thought Janice.

"She will get help doing the work. I'll have my bunkhouse cook prepare a nice meal. How about it, Janice?"

"Sure, Pa. I'll bake some apple-and-berry pies for dessert."

"Okay. Thank you for the invite. We never turn down a home-cooked meal. We'll all be back around dinnertime, Jesse. Nice to meet you, Miss

Janice," said TJ as he tipped his hat. The boys mounted and rode out toward town.

"Likewise, cowboy," she said. *I won't tell TJ how much I liked being on his lap and how it stirred me up about as much as I realized that sitting on his lap was getting him stirred up also. He has a lot more manners and class than his brother, Cimarron, although there is something very attractive and free-spirited or wild in Cimarron's character. Any girl that meets Cimarron gets the urge to want to rope him and tame down that spirit boy in him, kind of like the thrill of going after and capturing a wild stallion. It would be hard to choose between TJ and Cimarron. Their personalities are two different worlds apart, yet I really like them both. Even Sundell has that Lacey charm. I sure do hope they find Cimarron and that he is okay. It would be a disaster to lose one of the five brothers in Brawley. The Lacey clan would never forgive this town.*

CHAPTER VIII

THE DOUBLE D BAR RANCH

The Nevada Kid and Smokey trotted their horses up the long dirt road leading to the Double D Bar Ranch. They dismounted and tethered their horses at the rail in front of the long front porch of the ranch house. As they looked around at the ranch, they could see that Dan Donaldson managed to make a really good living out of the raw country he called the Double D Bar Ranch. The evidence was everywhere that he was justifiably proud and very deeply attached to the land that sustained him. The outbuildings and grazing areas were all fenced off from where the crops were grown. Nevada couldn't help but wonder where Dan Donaldson got all his money to keep this spread looking so prosperous and still growing.

"Pretty nice spread," whispered Smokey.

"Sure enough is," replied Nevada as he looked around.

They went up the front porch steps and knocked on the front door. A woman answered the door. "What can I do for you two gentlemen?" she asked.

"We are looking for Dan Donaldson, the man who owns this here spread. We would like to ask him a few questions. Where can we find him, ma'am?" said Nevada.

"Oh. My husband is in his study. He just finished his lunch, and he will be going back out on the range. I'll get him for you. Wait here, please." She closed the front door and left to get Dan. Nevada and Smokey looked at each other.

"Didn't even invite us in," said Nevada. "These people are not overly friendly."

"Guess it's not their way," replied Smokey.

The door opened again, and it was Dan Donaldson. He came out onto the porch and closed the door behind him as he did so.

"What can I do for you boys? You looking for work or something?"

"No, sir," said Nevada. "I'm looking for my son. He came to Brawley on business and never got back home. My name's Tom Lacey, and they call me the Nevada Kid. My son, Cimarron, disappeared somewhere between your ranch and the Bitter End Trail. I was wondering if someone on your ranch may have seen him pass through here or if you hired anyone new lately."

"Nobody has seen any strangers around here, and I didn't hire anyone new. I have all the regular ranch hands that I need, and most of them stay on all winter. Sorry, I can't help you. You better look somewhere else."

Just then, before Dan closed the door, a rider came up fast and dismounted. "Hey, Dan. You had this here telegram in town. I brought it back for you in case it's important."

"Thanks, Ace. Don't dillydally and get back to work."

"Okay, Dan," said Ace. Ace turned, facing Smokey and Nevada, and left.

Nevada gave Smokey a really hard look. Smokey knew exactly what Nevada's eyes were saying. He noticed it too. Ace was wearing a chain with a silver arrowhead on it. No mistaking it. It was Cimarron's neck chain. They never knew of any other one that looked exactly like that.

"Well, it's like I said, boys. I'm sorry I can't help you out. If I notice anything, I'll let you know. Where can I reach you in town?"

"We are staying at the Cattle Call Hotel on Main," said Nevada. "Much obliged, Mister Donaldson."

"Sorry I couldn't help you boys." He closed the front door hard in their faces.

"Nice guy," said Smokey. "He's not very friendly and seems to act like the sun comes up just to hear him crow." They mounted their horses.

"Sure enough. He's colder than a dead snake. Let's follow that guy Ace and see where he goes," said Nevada.

"He kind of got a good head start on us," said Smokey.

"Doesn't matter. Let's follow him anyway. He can't be going too far."

They followed Ace through the rangeland across the ranch property until they came to a gate in the fence. They passed through the gate, following a path into the woods for quite a ways, which brought them out onto, of all places, the Bitter End Trail where they lost him. They looked around hard but couldn't pick up his tracks.

"This is very interesting, Smokey," said Nevada. "The Bitter End Trail seems to border the Double D Bar Ranch land. It's easy to slip in and out of the Bitter End Trail from crossing this rangeland. Just pass through the gate in the fence and go over the rise, and in a couple of miles, you're on the Bitter End Trail."

"Wow! You got that right, Nevada. Are you thinking what I'm thinking?"

"Sure am, Smokey. These ranch hands could be robbing the stages and terrorizing the travelers on the Bitter End Trail. This gateway is an easy on and easy off passage to and from the trail. It must have been put here for a purpose by the Double D Bar ranch hands. I see no other real purpose for a gate in this part of the fence."

"I wonder where Ace disappeared to from here?"

"Don't know. Let's go back to town and meet up with the boys and see what they found out. There are a lot of shenanigans going on with this Double D Bar Ranch," said Nevada, "and I aim to find out just what they are. Let's mark this spot on the trail so we can find it again from the trail side."

Nevada dismounted and tied a piece of cheesecloth from his saddlebags on a tree branch where the pass through the woods came out and through to the trail. He bent down and picked something up off the ground three feet into the woods off the trail where they emerged: a package of genuine Bull Durham loose-leaf chewing tobacco. It was brand-new and yet to be opened. He held it up, showing it to Smokey.

"Isn't that the brand Cimarron chews?" replied Smokey.

"Sure is," said Nevada. "It's brand-new, not even opened yet. But it sure doesn't prove anything. It could belong to anybody." Nevada slipped the package into his pocket.

Since they were already on the Bitter End Trail, they followed it back to the stage route and then took the stage road back to town so as not to trespass across the Double D's pastures and rangeland again.

They arrived back in Brawley and went directly to the Branding Iron Saloon & Dance Hall. The four Lacey boys were at the round corner table, playing cards, as Smokey and Nevada joined them.

"Hey, Pa. The boot maker in town fixed the hole in my favorite boots. I won't have to buy another pair now," said Ty.

"Well, at least we got something accomplished in this worthless town," said Nevada. "So what did you boys find out at the telegraph office?" inquired Nevada.

"We found out that the town drunk sleeps on the bench out front of the office, along with other nosy townsfolk that hang out there," said Gage. Nevada frowned.

"We also found out that when Cimarron dictated the telegram message to the clerk, a Double D ranch hand named Ace was standing right behind him and heard the whole thing," said Ty.

Nevada exchanged glances with Smokey. "Sounds like this guy is our 'ace' in the hole, so to speak," said Nevada.

"He sure is, Nevada," replied Smokey.

"We ran into this guy Ace from the Double D delivering a telegram at the ranch this afternoon. We also noticed he was wearing Cimarron's silver neck chain," said Nevada.

"Are you serious, Pa?" said TJ.

"I wouldn't kid you about that, son. We also found out that the Double D ranchlands border the Bitter End Trail and has easy access on and off the trail from the grazing lands by about three miles. Where the pastures end, there's a gate in the fence where the woods start. The woods run in about two or three miles before you reach the Bitter End Trail. There is no reason for that fence gate to be where it is except to access the wooded trail."

Nevada reached in his pocket and threw the pack of chaw on the table. "Jeez, Ty, look at that! It's Cimarron's!" said Gage. "Where did you find it, Pa?"

"I found it in the woods about three yards from where we came out onto the Bitter End Trail. How do you know it's Cimarron's, Gage?"

"Because the store clerk said Cimarron bought a pack of Bull Durham chaw when he bought his supplies before leaving town!"

"Are you sure that's what he said?"

"Sure as shootin', Pa," replied Gage.

"This is serious, Pa," said Ty.

"You're dead right that it's serious. We may have discovered a venomous den of rattlesnakes that needs some serious cleaning out."

"What about Sundell and Ty? What did you two boys find out?" inquired Smokey.

"Well, for one thing, the whole transaction went along normal. Jesse Russell has a beautiful daughter that manages to get herself into fixes all the time." TJ laughed. "She did a good number on me and managed to get me aroused."

"Yeah," laughed Sundell. "Cimarron sang love songs to her on the veranda after he had dinner there. She said she was on that stagecoach coming back from Arizona when it got robbed, and Cimarron interrupted the robbery and saved her life. He drove the stage into town with the driver and shotgun guard dead inside the coach. She rode on top in the driver's seat with him, and he had his horses tied onto the back of the stagecoach. She said she insulted him and said he had a rank-horse stink on him." Sundell and TJ started laughing. "It seems she doesn't cotton to dirty, stinking men." Sundell looked at TJ and again started laughing.

"That sounds like she met up with our horse-toting Cimarron, all right," said Nevada. He turned and looked at Sundell. "You boys got some kind of a dirty private joke you're laughing at?" replied Nevada.

"I guess you could call it that, Pa" Sundell laughed harder, slamming his fist on the table.

"Enough of that, Sundell," said TJ. "After Cimarron left the ranch that night, Jesse never saw or heard of him again. But, Pa, Jesse offered us his ranch hands to help in the search."

"Yeah, and we are all invited there for a home-cooked dinner tonight," said Sundell. "Can we go, Pa?"

"Sure can," said Nevada. "I'll need to see Jesse and brief him on everything we found out today. Let's head back to the hotel and get cleaned up for dinner. We sure as hell don't want any of us smelling like our horses at the dinner table."

~~~T2~~~

When Nevada, Smokey, and the four Lacey brothers walked their horses up to the veranda of Jesse Russell's ranch house, Janice lost her breath, causing her to unconsciously drop her needlework on the porch floor in front of her rocker as she stood up. This was one family of gorgeous-looking men! Clean-shaven, combed hair, all of them wearing Stetsons and clean, polished leather boots. Three of them had leather vests on; two of them wore silver chains around their necks, but no Indian arrowheads like Cimarron had on his chain. If she had to pick one and say he appealed to her the most as the cleanest and most prominent-looking rancher, she couldn't pick one out because they all appealed to her equally, even the two older seasoned cowboys. She was dazed over seeing so many good-looking men in one group and all of them wearing their guns hanging low and tied down like the fast gunmen they were all trained to be. In fact, she was so dazed that she didn't notice TJ dismount and come up on the porch until he bent down, picked up, and handed her the needlework she dropped. It was then she snapped out of her daze.

"Oh my gosh! Thank you, TJ," she said. "You men are right on time too."

"Yes, ma'am," replied Nevada. *She is beautiful,* he thought. *My boys are in for some big trouble tonight. No wonder they were so anxious to clean up and come back here for dinner.* They dismounted and tethered their horses to the rail in front of the house. As they came up the porch steps to join TJ and Janice, TJ made the introductions, and it was then that Jesse came out the door and greeted them.

"The Nevada Kid! Damn, it's been years since I've seen you last, kid." Jesse offered his hand to shake, then grabbed Nevada, giving him a hug. Then he shook Smokey's hand. "How have you two boys been?"

"We're keeping busy, Jesse, with ranch work," replied Nevada.

"Wow, you got yourself a fine family of boys here. Any of your boys doing the rodeo circuit yet?"

"Not yet, Jesse. Maybe Cimarron will get into it soon," said Nevada.

"Cimarron. That's right. That's why you are here. Dinner is coming out on the table. Let's go on in and sit down and eat. We will discuss Cimarron during dinner. I hope you boys like hickory-smoked beef."

"Yes, sir. We surely do, Jesse," said Nevada.

"Nevada, remember, you're the one that showed me how to hickory smoke beef. You got me started on it, and I've done it ever since." Nevada laughed.

The dishes and casseroles were brought out and passed around the table family style. The aroma of fresh baked bread and berry pies filled the air as they were placed on the table. When Janice approached the table and was ready to sit down, all the boys stood up out of respect, and TJ pulled out her chair so she could sit down. Janice was thrilled. She felt as if she was in seventh heaven. All this respect from all these good-looking young cowboys. She hardly knew what to say. She barely could get a thank-you out.

Everyone was chowing down the beef, when Janice suddenly asked TJ, "So, TJ, you are the oldest. Is there someone special in your life? You have your own ranch house and all, so Ty said."

"No, Miss Janice. I'm not married, and I have no girlfriend, I'm sorry to say. I had a girl back East when I was in college. She didn't like the desert, she didn't like the smell of cattle and horses, and she just plainly didn't like ranching. Wanted me to stay back East and be a city attorney, and it just wasn't for me. When I left to come home to my ranch, she broke my heart, just didn't come with me. I've been alone ever since."

"I'm sorry to hear that, TJ. You must be lonesome. But I'm sure a nice man like you will find someone really soon."

TJ didn't answer. The Lacey boys just exchanged glances, looking at each other, smiling without saying a word.

"TJ will make a good husband for some really nice girl when he is ready," replied Nevada. Smokey just giggled.

"What about Cimarron?" questioned Janice. "Does he have a special girl?"

"Janice, behave yourself," said her father. "Stop asking the boys personal questions."

"Cimarron?" said Sundell in surprise. All the brothers started laughing.

Janice wasn't quite sure what the joke was. "Yes," she said. "Cimarron."

"Well, you see, Miss Janice," TJ explained. "Cimarron is 100 percent cowboy and a drifter. He is a horse whisperer, and he will never settle down. He is exactly like the wild stallion you see out on the plains. Everywhere he goes, there is a remuda of wild mares running after him. Not one has been able to catch him yet. He is as free as a raven on the wing. I don't ever see him settling down for any reason. Cimarron is quite the charmer when it comes to females. He lets them get just close enough, and when they turn around, he's gone. He's the kind of wild-spirit boy a nice girl has to watch out for, if you know what I mean. As a matter of fact, I can't wait to see what kind of girl is gonna throw a rope over his mane, keep him penned, and ride him down to a trot long enough to tame him. It would be some kind of woman that can do that!"

Laughter resounded all around the table. "You're too nice a girl to get involved with the wild beast in Cimarron," said Sundell.

"I don't know about that," interrupted Smokey. "Your father, the Nevada Kid, was the exact same way when your mother, Ricki, the barrel racer, took him down. He was helpless when she went after him. She gave him such a hard time he refused to quit chasing her until he finally got her—or until she rode him down."

"Okay, Smokey. That's enough. You're getting too technical," said Nevada.

"I don't know. I think the boys ought to know how Ricki trapped you. It's a great story, Nevada," laughed Smokey.

"Yeah, with a lot of help from you. Let's get back to Cimarron. That's what we are here for," said Nevada.

Nevada informed Jesse of all the information he and the boys found out about the Double D Bar Ranch and its ranch hands. Nevada also revealed that he had found and picked up a small package of genuine Bull Durham loose-leaf chewing tobacco, which was dropped along the trail where they came out onto the Bitter End Trail from the Double D Bar Ranch. That was Cimarron's favorite brand of chaw. Could it be that Cimarron dropped it while he was possibly abducted or taken away?

"You know, Nevada, the Double D has a few line shacks along its borderline. It might not be a bad idea to check out those line shacks. You never know, maybe Ace disappeared to one of them," said Jesse.

"How many do you think there are, Jesse?" replied Nevada.

"Well, now, let me see. I know there are three heading east along the property line, but I don't know if there are any in the other direction going west."

"Pa," interrupted Janice. "I believe there is one heading west along the borderline, but it is no longer used. I think they abandoned it."

"Well, now, how did you know about that one, Janice?" queried Jesse.

"I'd rather not say, Pa." She flushed with embarrassment. "But I saw it once, a long time ago when I was riding that way with one of the Double D cowhands."

"What cowhand? The one you were dating that I couldn't stand and wanted you to get rid of?" replied Jesse, a bit irritated.

"That wasn't necessary, Pa. I was just trying to help," said Janice.

"Well, you and I will discuss this again later, young lady," said Jesse. Janice just rolled her eyes to the ceiling. The Laceys kept quiet and stayed out of this family argument. TJ's thoughts found it to be amusing. *Jesse must have caught Janice slipping around with some cowhand he didn't approve of,* he laughed to himself.

"Tell you what," said Nevada. "We'll head east and check out the three line shacks there first."

"I'll go with you, Nevada, and bring some of my ranch hands," said Jesse. "We'll meet you first thing in the morning on the stage road out of town."

"Sounds like a plan, Jesse. I'm much obliged."

~~~**T2**~~~

It was late evening when the Lacey boys had gone back to town, and Janice's father, Jesse, went to bed. Janice quietly slipped out of her room and out to the corral to saddle her horse. She was determined to check out the abandoned line shack where she used to sneak off with Tucker, one of the ranch hands from the Double D Bar Ranch. It was a few days ago that she heard and saw some riders heading off in that direction, and she wondered where they were going. She decided it was time to check that area out. Jesse would never approve of this action, and she knew it, so she decided to take care of it herself.

When she approached the line shack, to her great surprise, it was being occupied. Smoke was coming from the chimney, and the glow of lamps coming from the windows could be noticed. Horses showed restlessness in the nearby pole corral. She decided to sneak up unnoticed to a window and peek in to see who it was that occupied the shack. Three of the Double D ranch hands were familiar to her, but two of the other men were not. Janice quietly watched through the window and listened to their conversation. *Why, they're discussing the stagecoach robbery!* she thought. Were these the outlaws that robbed the stage she was riding? Were the Double D ranch hands in on the robbery? She just couldn't believe what she was hearing. She could not see into the back storage room because there were no windows in it. One of the men went in there to check on something and came back out. "He's still out cold" was his reply.

Oh my gosh! thought Janice. *Is it possible they have Cimarron as a prisoner in there?*

Suddenly, someone came up behind her and put his hand over her mouth, grabbing her around the waist and lifting her off the ground.

"Well, if it isn't Janice Russell! What the hell are you doing here, spying on us? Let's go inside and see what the boys think about this," said Luke. He dragged her around to the front door of the cabin and literally threw her through the door. She stumbled and fell on the floor. "Look what I found outside peering in through the side window, boys."

"I thought maybe Tucker was here, and I came to see him," Janice stuttered.

"Don't give me that shit," said Ace. "You and Tucker broke up a couple of months ago. Tucker isn't here because he is not in on this deal. Now what are you doing around here this late at night?" That is when Janice noticed Cimarron's neck chain on Ace, just as his father, Nevada, had mentioned.

"It's like I said, Ace. I'm looking for Tucker. We used to meet here."

"Bad answer, Janice. You're lying. Tie her hands behind her back, boys, and throw her in the back room with Cimarron. Now we have two bodies to get rid of, boys. Darn our bad luck," said Ace.

"Do we have to kill her, Ace?" said Cullen.

"What do you expect? She heard everything, and she is also a witness to the stage robbery. She's leaving us no choice!" said Ace. "This girl can get herself into more trouble than a wet dog at a parlor social. She left us no choice but to deal with her. I don't like this either." They tied her hands and put her in the back room with Cimarron as she struggled from the hold on her. She heard enough to realize her worst fears.

"Well, then, let's just divide the money and run. We got the stage money and the money off the Cimarron Kid. We'll head for a border town," said Cullen.

"Can't do that," said John Spence. "Cimarron killed my brother, Dave, and it's an eye for an eye. He is not getting away with that. He dies, and so does she."

"Jeez, John. He is almost dead now, with the beating he took and all," said Cullen. "Can't we just leave them here?"

"No. I don't want any witnesses. The girl was a witness to the stage robbery. Let's get some shut-eye tonight, and we'll take care of these two sometime tomorrow."

"Help! Help!" Janice was screaming.

"What the devil is the matter with you?" said Cullen, peeking in the door of the back room.

"Cut me loose. Cimarron is in trouble. He needs help. He's hurt bad. Please let me take care of him so he doesn't die tonight."

"Are you crazy or something? You're both goin' to die tomorrow. If he died tonight, it will save us the trouble of getting rid of him tomorrow."

"Please, Cullen. You got to give me a canteen of water and let me help him. I will be grateful to you. You just can't let him suffer and die like this."

"Okay. But you got to promise me one thing. You will not try and get away if I cut you loose. You just take care of him, and nothing else. The boss will kill me if you try anything or get away."

"I swear, I promise. I'll just take care of him. Please, Cullen."

Cullen came in with a canteen full of cold water and set it down. He cut the ropes binding Janice, and she immediately tore up some cloth and wet it down. She dabbed at Cimarron's dry, parched lips and gave him a trickle of water in his mouth. She placed a cold compress on his head and washed the blood and dirt from his swollen, bruised face. Cullen left the room. It didn't look like Janice would leave Cimarron alone for even a minute. He knew her well enough to know he could trust her. She was a warmhearted, compassionate girl. Besides, there was no window in that back storage room for her to escape. She wasn't going anywhere too soon. Taking care of that beat-up horse wrangler would keep her busy for a while and out of trouble.

Janice knew full well that as soon as her father found her missing, they would all be looking for her. If she could only keep Cimarron alive long enough for his father and brothers to find them and get him to a doctor. It was worth every effort she could do to save him. She only hoped one thing: that her father would remember she'd told them all at dinner about the abandoned line shack west of the Double D Bar Ranch where she and Tucker used to slip off to and meet. It was her last hope that they remembered. She had to do everything she could to keep Cimarron alive until the others got there. It was possible Cimarron was suffering from a concussion by the looks of the cut and swelled-up large lump on the back of his head. They must have hit him from behind with something very hard to do that to him. She prayed that he wasn't bleeding internally. This is one time she hoped this cowboy's stubborn hardheadedness was to his advantage.

They gave her a bowl of stew to eat for supper, not knowing she ate earlier at home. She fed the gravy and soupy liquid part of it to Cimarron with her spoon. She was surprised he was able to swallow it down. There may be some hope for him yet. *Please get here soon,* she thought. They just have to get here and save him from these cruel men. He was slightly conscious while he sipped the gravy and then drifted back to sleep with his head on her lap. She kept putting cold, wet compresses to his head to reduce any swelling. It seemed to be helping. There wasn't a whole lot more she could do for him.

Chapter IX

THE SKIRMISH

The search party searched all three line shacks along the eastern border of the Double D spread and found nothing in them. Jesse Russell and his ranch hands helped with the search. They decided to double back to Jesse's spread using the Bitter End Trail. Halfway back to Jesse's ranch, they met one of his drovers riding at lightning speed up to meet them. He pulled up short and was almost breathless.

"Boss, Janice is missing!"

"What do you mean 'Janice is missing'?" asked Jesse.

"Well, boss. She must have ridden out sometime during the night to help search for Cimarron!"

"What? And nobody saw her or stopped her? She rode out alone, you fools?" said Jesse.

"Well, nobody saw her leave, boss. Her horse was gone this morning, and she is missing. You know how Janice is, boss. She must have left during the night, and no one noticed until after you all left this morning on the search. When she sets her mind to doing something, she just does it."

"That means she has been gone all night or more. Which direction did she ride off into? Do you know?" inquired Jesse.

"I guess I would say west, boss. She must have gone to the opposite direction as you and the search party. Her horse's tracks were headed west."

"Jesse," said Nevada. "Remember she said there was an abandoned line shack on the west border of the Double D Bar Ranch? Let's go find it. What can we lose if we check that out too? We'll help you find her."

"All right, Nevada. Jake, go to town and get the sheriff and a posse to help us. Tell him what happened. Catch up with us on the west border of the Double D spread. Let's go, boys! We're looking for an abandoned line shack possibly being used on the border of the Double D spread!" yelled Jesse. They all turned their horses and headed out in search of the line shack.

They rode along for about a half hour or more, when someone spotted smoke rising from a lone shack beyond the wooded area. They dismounted and walked their horses closer to the shack to get a better look. Next to the shack was a corral of horses, which looked to be holding about a dozen horses; a few of them were still saddled.

"Now that is no abandoned line shack," whispered Jesse.

"Gage," said Nevada. "Gather all our horses and stay with them. Hobble them and make sure they don't startle and run away."

"But, Pa—" argued Gage.

"Don't question me. Just do it!"

"Aw, Pa," said Gage. "If there's gonna be shooting, I want in on it." He took the reins of all the horses, keeping them quiet and walking them out of sight, away from the line shack.

Nevada, Jesse, and the search party quietly slipped up to the line shack. Nevada whispered to Jesse, "I'll slip up to that window and take out that guard near the corner. Maybe I can see or hear what's going on and who is in there."

"Okay, Nevada, but be careful," said Jesse. "Wait here, boys, until Nevada gets back."

Nevada slipped up behind the guard and buffaloed him with the butt of his gun, knocking him out cold. He slipped up to the window and peeked in. It was the Double D ranch hands, all right; Ace and Cullen were with them. But where was Janice or Cimarron? They were not in the room. He hoped he was not too late. They were already counting out money to divide it up among them. Then Cullen said, "I'll bring the girl something to eat," as he took the ladle in the stewpot and filled a plate with stew. He went in through a door leading to a small storage room, carrying the plate of food in his hand. Nevada heard the sound of a woman's voice. *That must be Janice in there,* he thought. *At least we found her.* Cullen came back out of the storage room.

"Well, I just gave her the last meal. When do we get rid of the Cimarron Kid and the girl? Tomorrow?"

Nevada held his breath. Was it possible that Cimarron was still alive and in that back storage room with Janice? Did he hear that last statement right? He listened some more to the conversations. They were laughing and joking about how they robbed the Cimarron Kid of fifteen hundred dollars in ranch money. Then they talked about the stage robbery and then how they would head for the border as soon as Donaldson gave them their wages. They were planning on running out and leaving the Double D short on hands. The worse thing they could do to any rancher: they were quitting on the brand they rode for and riding out just before a cattle drive. *Not on my watch,* thought Nevada. He slipped back to join the group in the search party. Sheriff Williams quietly arrived with his posse to join them, leaving their horses with Gage. He slipped up next to Nevada and Jesse and listened in on the conversation.

"Hi, sheriff. Janice and Cimarron are in the back storage room of this shack. There are no windows in that storage room, so we have to go in through the front door of the shack. We got no choice. Have your men and the posse totally surround the line shack. Let me know when they are in place. I counted twelve inside the shack and one outside on guard, whom I knocked out. Listen up, men. Do not, under any circumstances, fire any shots at that back storage room. We can't take a chance on stray bullets going through the wallboards and hitting Janice or Cimarron. Does everybody understand that?"

"Yes," they all whispered.

"Okay," said Nevada. "Smokey, TJ, Ty, Sundell, and I will defend the front of the shack. Sheriff Williams and Jesse, you take one side each of the shack with your men."

So they took their positions, and Nevada waited for the signal from Jesse and the sheriff that the men were in place.

"Hello in the shack!" yelled Nevada. "Come out with your hands up and don't touch any of your guns. We have you surrounded, so come out peacefully."

No answer came back, but the shack went silent, and the lamps were blown out. From out of the darkness came a voice. "Who are you and what do you want?"

"It's Tom Lacey, Jesse Russell, Sheriff Williams, and a posse. Now come out peacefully with your hands up. You are all under arrest for robbery, murder, and kidnapping. We have you surrounded."

"Tom Lacey? Why, you are the Nevada Kid! We aren't coming out kid," said John Spence. "You gone loco or something? Why are you on the side of law enforcement? You should be in here, working with us, with your reputation for a fast gun. Something wrong with your brains, Kid?"

"There's nothing wrong with my brains, but there is something wrong with yours. You got my son, Cimarron, in there, and I want him back. So hold your hands high if you expect to go on living, and all of you come out here, *now!*"

"You heard him, John. You are all under arrest. This is Sheriff Williams. Surrender and come out. We have you surrounded. You don't stand a chance."

"Hell! Cimarron is your kid, Nevada? I didn't know that. I hate to tell you this, but he had a little bit of an accident and ain't doin' so well. He was putting up resistance with the boys and sort of got himself roughened up. The boys just couldn't take his kind of rowdy manner. Ha ha ha!"

"You do any permanent harm to my kid, and I'll kill you all myself, you snakes in the grass. Now come out with your hands up before I really get agitated. All of you."

"You want your kid, you come in and get him, but you got to go through us first, you turncoat outlaw." John broke a window and fired out of it. Nevada shot back as gunfire erupted, on three sides, around the cabin.

When Janice heard the gunfire, she quickly gathered storage boxes and pushed them all around herself and Cimarron to protect them from any stray bullets. She put Cimarron's head in her lap and ducked down lower than the storage boxes, keeping them both protected by the surrounding boxes.

The volleys of gunfire continued around the line shack for what seemed like hours to Janice. Every once in a while, she would hear someone yell out when they were hit with a bullet or a stray shot, until at last, the sounds gradually began to diminish. Janice could hear only three gunmen left firing out of the shack and talking back and forth to each other. Suddenly, the door of the shack was kicked open, slamming against the back wall. Two more gunshots inside the shack this time as Nevada and Smokey were defending themselves.

"Okay, drop that gun," said Nevada.

"You're the Nevada Kid?" said John Spence.

"That's right," said Nevada. "What's your name?"

"I'm John Spence, you bastard. Your kid shot my brother!"

"As I heard it from the sheriff, it was self-defense," replied Nevada. "Your brother provoked the fight and drew first."

"Doesn't matter. My brother is still dead, you ornery coyote."

"You are lucky I'm letting you live long enough to do your hanging around on a rope, Spence," said Nevada.

Just then, the sheriff and Jesse Russell came in through the line shack door. The sheriff cuffed John Spence and helped him up off the floor. Then he cuffed two other wounded outlaws.

"Let's go, John. You boys are under arrest for murder, robbery, and kidnapping. Too bad most of your gang never lived long enough to make it to a trial," said Sheriff Williams. "Robbing the mail from the stage is a serious federal offense. You three will get a fair trial. You're in big trouble though, because murder is a hanging offense. You murdered the stage driver and the guard."

Smokey reached down and took Cimarron's neck chain off Ace's dead body. He handed it to Nevada. Nevada looked at it and put it in his pocket. Smokey and Nevada turned and went into the back room and up to Janice, whom they found sitting on the floor behind some boxes with Cimarron's head cradled on her lap.

"Are you okay, Janice?" questioned Nevada.

"Yes, I am," she replied. She was trembling in fear. "But I'm afraid Cimarron is in big trouble. I suspect he has a concussion."

"Either of you get hit with any stray bullets?" questioned Smokey.

"No, Smokey. We are fine. I protected us with the storage boxes."

"That was quick thinking," replied Nevada. "You are a smart girl."

Smokey helped her stand up on her feet just as Jesse was coming in through the door. Jesse took hold of her and hugged her, then helped her walk out into the main room. Sheriff Williams was walking John Spence and two of his gang, handcuffed, out the door to the horses where Gage was leading them all up to the shack. Nevada and Smokey pushed the boxes aside and bent down over Cimarron to check him out. The Kid was out cold and was breathing very shallow. Janice's cold compresses were keeping the swelling down. The four Lacey boys came rushing into the room, stopping short. They were all standing very silently, just staring at their father, Nevada, holding Cimarron in his arms.

"He's alive," whispered Smokey to the boys. The Lacey boys passed glances around at each other.

"He needs a doctor fast," said Nevada. "He may have a concussion. There is dried blood on his head where he was hit hard with a blunt instrument. Probably a gun butt or barrel. It could probably use stitches where the bleeding clotted in the open wound."

"Ty, Gage," said TJ. "I saw an old fence supply wagon on the other side of the shack. Hook up some horses and bring it around the front. We'll put him in there and take him into town. Pa, you hold him and sit with him in the wagon."

"Good idea," said Smokey. "Nevada, I'll help you carry him out. Sundell, you ride ahead into town with the sheriff and his posse and get the doc. Bring him over to the hotel and have him there when we arrive with Cimarron. Where is Jesse?"

"Jesse and his men are taking Janice back to the Pinion Pine Ranch. She has some scrapes and bruises that need attention but not bad enough to need the doc," said Sundell. "She is gonna be all right. She is shaken up more n' anything—and worried over Cimarron."

"Well, then. Let's take care of Cimarron. TJ, help us get him out onto that wagon," said Smokey.

Sundell did a flying mount onto his horse and headed back to town with the posse to fetch the doctor.

"Smokey, I'm gonna kill that bastard, John Spence, with my own two hands, if this boy dies. Laws or no laws, I don't give a shit. I'll turn Spence's ass to dust. Damn these baboons."

"It's okay, Nevada. They are gonna get justice. Let's take care of the Kid right now. He needs us more 'n anything."

The rickety wagon pulled up in front of the line shack, with Ty at the reins and Gage in the seat next to him. Their horses were already tied on the back of the wagon. Nevada, Smokey, and TJ gently lifted Cimarron into the wagon, and Nevada got in with him. Smokey tied Nevada's horse on the back of the wagon, next to the other two horses, and mounted his own.

The old supply wagon gently followed the crooked, winding trail back to the stagecoach road. TJ and Smokey rode back to town alongside the wagon. The wagon rolled slowly and easily as it bumped along the dirt stagecoach road back to Brawley. They pulled up in front of the Cattle Call Hotel and stopped. Gage jumped out of the wagon, ran into the hotel, and ran up to the desk.

"We got Cimarron outside in a wagon. Is his room still open? We need a place to put him up and where the doc can take care of him," said Gage.

"Go ahead and put him in room 10. Nobody is assigned to that room yet," replied the clerk. Gage ran back outside.

"Put him up in room 10, his old room, again. The clerk said it's still open," said Gage.

Smokey, TJ, and Nevada carried Cimarron upstairs to room number 10, his old room, and put him in bed as Sundell, with the doctor at his heels, came in through the door behind them.

"Okay. Everybody clear the room while I examine him and make a determination. I don't want anybody in my way," said Doc.

The Lacey boys waited in the hallway for more than an hour for the doctor to come out and give them a verdict. They all gathered around him when he finally came out of the room.

"Well, Doc. What's the story?" said Nevada.

"I really can't say," said Doc.

"What do you mean you can't say?" questioned Nevada.

"Just what I said," replied Doc. "He is in a semicoma, and I won't know anything until he wakes up and comes out of the coma. I can tell you this though. He suffered a concussion. He has three broken ribs, which is causing labored breathing, and face lacerations, so I know he was punched in the face, but I don't know if it was before or after the concussion. I put seventeen stitches on his scalp where someone buffaloed him on the back of the head with the butt of a gun. This boy's body is in shock. This young man is fighting for his life right now. All we can do now is to wait and see if he wakes up and comes out of that shock. How long that will be, well, we have no way of knowing. As soon as he stirs or wakes up, if he does, come and get me right away, especially if you see any change in him."

"Sure thing, Doc," said Nevada in a soft, sad voice.

They all went back into Cimarron's room, leaving the hallway empty. Nevada sat down on a chair next to Cimarron's bed. About a half hour later, Smokey said, "C'mon, boys, let's go get a drink at the saloon. We can't do anything more here. Nevada, we'll bring you something back to eat and drink."

"I'm not hungry, Smokey."

"We'll do it anyway," replied Smokey. "Maybe you'll be hungry later on."

They left Nevada alone in the room and headed down to the saloon and dance hall. Nevada was tired and restless, but he could not sleep. He reached in his pocket and took out Cimarron's silver neck chain. He stared at the pure silver arrowhead for a minute. Then he lifted Cimarron's head and looped the chain over it, putting the neck chain back on. Now his son looked like the Cimarron Kid again. He rested his own head back against the wall and, suddenly and unexpectedly, dozed off to sleep.

~~~T2~~~

Smokey and the Lacey boys headed down the boardwalk to the Branding Iron Saloon & Dance Hall. As soon as they entered, Jennifer ran over to them.

"I heard you brought Cimarron in. How is he? Please tell me. I gotta know."

"Well," said Smokey. "The doc just left, and his pa is with him right now. He is hurt pretty bad. Doc put seventeen stitches on his head where the outlaws hit him hard with a gun butt. He is in shock. Possibly a semicoma. The Kid is fighting for his life, trying to stay alive. You got a fresh deck of cards we can use while we are waiting for him to wake up? No telling how long that will be."

"Yes," said Jennifer. "I'll get you a deck. What will y'all drink?"

"Beers all around the table," said Smokey.

"I'll get them right away," said Jennifer.

They were into a game of poker when the saloon was interrupted by Mr. Donaldson, with two of his hired hands, coming through the batwing doors. He was not a happy fellow. His cold eyes would chill a side of beef. He came up to the bar and ordered three whiskeys. He drank his whiskey down fast and ordered another. Then he turned and addressed the patrons in the bar.

"I'll need about ten new hands on my ranch, if anybody is interested in signing up. Lost half of my ranch hands in a shoot-out. I'm sure you all heard about it by now. The pay is thirty dollars a month and found. Anybody that signs up better be straight, or I'll damn well shoot him myself and not wait for the sheriff to do it. Now how many of you want jobs working for the Double D Bar Ranch?"

The poker game momentarily halted as Smokey and the Lacey boys listened in. About three drovers came forward to the bar. "We'll sign up. We need jobs, Mr. Donaldson," said one of them.

"That's it? Only three of you?" replied Mr. Donaldson. "I got a cattle drive coming up and need more hands."

"Okay. We'll sign up too," said two more cowboys walking forward to the bar.

"Get their names and sign them up, Tucker," said Mr. Donaldson. "That makes only five replacements, and I said I needed ten. Ain't there five more of you that want jobs and are willing to work? How about you boys sitting over there in the corner? Anybody interested in work?" He was addressing the Lacey family.

Smokey pushed his chair back, stood up, turned, and faced Mr. Donaldson. "We got jobs with the Flying T2 Brand out of Yuma. We don't want anything you have to offer, Mr. Donaldson." He crossed his arms, giving Donaldson a stern look.

"I know you," said Mr. Donaldson. "You were at my ranch the other day with another fellow, two gunslingers asking questions. You're the two that started this whole mess and got my hands all shot up."

"Your hands were outlaws, Mr. Donaldson. They were robbing the stagecoaches and the mail in this area. They were looting travelers on the Bitter End Trail and are also murderers. You don't care who you hire or who works for you."

"That's not true, mister. I had no idea what they were doing. You just heard me say I'll shoot anybody that signs up that ain't straight."

"Well, then, maybe you should have checked on them sooner than this. I suppose you're gonna say you didn't know about the extra gate at the end of your grazing lands that leads into the woods and out onto the Bitter End Trail. Your hands buffaloed the brother of these here four boys and left him in the back room of an abandoned line shack, on your spread, *dying*. Cimarron has seventeen stitches on his head and is lying in a coma, fighting for his life right now. If we lose this twenty-year-old boy, there will be hell to pay for those bastards in that jail. They also robbed Cimarron and split up our ranch money. Who's gonna replace the lost ranch money they stole from us? You?"

"What happened to him ain't my fault. He killed my foreman's brother down at the corral and one of my ranch hands in the hotel. He was a fast gun. He doesn't deserve to live."

"That's a lie, you no-good polecat! It was self-defense both times, and you know it. Ask the sheriff. There were witnesses."

"I heard what happened." Donaldson's eyes were as cold as the stare from a Gila monster. With those words, the Lacey boys all stood up around the table, joining Smokey, posing a serious threat, very obviously unhooking the thongs from their guns. Mr. Donaldson got nervous and was ready to back down, when the sheriff walked into the saloon, interrupting the argument.

"All right. What's going on in here? Everybody keep your hands off your guns and settle down. Mr. Donaldson, I want you over at my office for some questioning. I heard you were in town. Let's go now. I don't want any trouble with this Lacey gang hanging out here, and I need some answers from you on your three boys in my jail. Let's go. You Lacey boys sit down and behave yourselves."

"All right, sheriff. I'll come. You boys whose names Tucker just took, report to my ranch early tomorrow morning with your gear," said Dave Donaldson. "Move into the bunkhouse and be ready to work at sunup." Mr. Donaldson left the saloon with the sheriff. He was glad to be out of the tense atmosphere and a little breathless from the fear of a showdown with the fast young guns of the Lacey family.

~~~T2~~~

I was so glad when I opened up my eyes and did not hear any harp music or see anyone playing a harp. This room that I'm in looks very familiar.

Now I remember. It's my room at the Cattle Call Hotel. How did I get in here? Was I dreaming the whole time when I was thinking I left for home early this morning? I turned over and got a horrible pain in my ribs, which caused me to groan and clutch my side. My head hurt somewhat fiercely too. When I touched my head, I groaned again, because as I felt it, it was wrapped with bandages, and I could feel a tight pinching on my scalp. A movement next to me caused me to look over and see my Pa waking up on a chair next to the bed.

"Jeez, Pa. Where did you come from?"

"I came from Yuma, looking for you, you wise-guy kid. Thank God you finally woke up!"

"Woke up? How long have I been out?"

"I'd say at least five days or more. You got buffaloed with the butt of a gun, and Doc put seventeen stitches on your scalp! You are lucky to be alive. Those outlaws kicked you in the ribs and broke three ribs on you too."

"Crap! No wonder I'm feeling so rotten and in so much pain. How did I get back here in my hotel room?"

"Long story. Smokey, your brothers, and I brought you back in a supply wagon from an old line shack on the Double D Bar Ranch. Lucky for you, those outlaws captured and held Janice Russell, or we would never have found you before they killed you. You got Janice to thank for still being alive. She held them off from killing you and her, and she also took care of you, keeping you alive until we got there to save you both and get you out. You missed one hell of a good shootout!"

"What about the ranch money, Pa? What happened to it?"

"They robbed you and split up the money. It's gone, son. Nothing more we can do about it. Most of it got spent."

"Jeez, Pa. I'm so sorry about that. I'll pay you back, I promise. You can take it out of my pay."

"If I take it out of your pay, cowboy, it will take you forty years to pay me back. Forget it, son. The money is lost. We are lucky we still got you. Even that was sketchy for quite a while. We'll make up the money in some other way. Right now, my priority is getting you back home safely and getting that last cattle drive north before the snow flies." There was a knock on the room door. "C'mon in," replied Nevada.

The doc walked in to do his routine check and was surprised to find Cimarron awake and talking. He winked at Nevada. "This is good news to see the boy awake. It should be an uphill recovery now, Nevada."

Nevada breathed a sigh of relief and shook his head. "He just woke up, Doc. I was gonna come and get you. While you're checking him over, Doc, I'll go down to the saloon and tell the boys Cimarron's awake if they want to see him and talk to him."

"Okay, Nevada. But I'd be careful if I were you. I heard Dave Donaldson is in town, looking for new hands to hire, and he's not too happy about the outcome at his line shack. He got a good grouchy disposition going on."

"Well, when you hire outlaws to work for you, you got to deal with it and suffer the results when judgment time comes down the trail. I'll be right back, Doc. Thanks for the warning."

Nevada went down to the saloon to get Smokey and his boys and to inform them of the good news that Cimarron woke up from his deep sleep. On their way back up the boardwalk, Dave Donaldson came out of the sheriff's office just as Nevada and the boys were close to passing by the door. They stopped short on the boardwalk as Donaldson confronted Nevada. Both men dropped their hands to their sidearms.

"Where do you think you are going, Nevada?" replied Dave Donaldson.

"I got a family to round up and to herd on back home and a ranch to run in Yuma, Dave. What seems to be your problem?"

"You're like a tick in my hide that I can't scratch out, Nevada. You stepped on my toes, trespassed on my land, destroyed my line shack, and shot up half of my ranch hands. You got a lot of sand in your craw, asking me what seems to be *my* problem."

"Your ranch hands had it coming, Donaldson. They were all outlaws! Now get out of my way, or I'll go right through you. I've had a belly full of fighting battles for the town of Brawley. From now on, these people better cure their own troubles and leave my family out of it."

"You got a lot of balls, calling my hands outlaws when you lived with and rode with the worst bunch of scorpions in the desert. You were always one gallop ahead of the law. Now you got my foreman and two of my drovers in jail with hanging offenses on them. The sooner you and your fast-gunning brood get the hell out of this town, the better I'll like it."

"Good. So get out of my way, Donaldson, and we'll make your dream come true."

Just then, the sheriff came out of his office. "All right," said the sheriff. "Let's not start anything up, you two. Donaldson, cross the street and be on your way. Nevada, finish up your business and get out of my town. I don't want any more trouble from anybody."

Dave Donaldson frowned and crossed the street, walking down the boardwalk on the other side.

"We'll be leaving pronto, sheriff. Cimarron woke up. Doc is with him now, and as soon as we know he can ride, we'll all be gone. How's that sound?"

"Isn't soon enough to suit me. By the way, thank you for cleaning out that nest of outlaws for me. Hopefully, when we meet again, it will be under better circumstances. You boys need not say good-bye to me when you leave. Just get out of town and get out of my sight."

"I hear you, sheriff, and I get your message loud and clear. Let's go, boys, and finish up our business and put this town behind us." They all walked down to the Cattle Call Hotel. Nevada stopped at the desk, while the others climbed the stairs and went to see Cimarron.

"Write up my bill, mister. We are leaving in the morning. Two boys will be staying in room 10 for a few more days, and they will pay you for whatever they run up in expenses from tomorrow morning until they leave. Are you in agreement with that?"

"Yes, sir, Mr. Nevada. I'll have your bill ready when you come down in the morning, and I'll separately bill room 10 for however long they stay starting tomorrow. How's that?"

"Perfect." Nevada left and went upstairs to Cimarron's room. He stopped in the hall and talked to Doc as the doc was just leaving.

"What do I owe you, Doc?"

"Let's see, Nevada. I guess ten dollars should cover everything. If you're planning on leaving soon, I wouldn't put that young man on a horse for three days yet."

"Okay, Doc. Thanks for everything," replied Nevada. He offered a handshake, and Doc took it. He walked into the room at the end of a conversation the boys were having with Cimarron. There were lots of giggles and laughter going on among the boys.

"Yeah. So there he was, staring at the painting of the nude pinup over the bar, while Pa was trying to introduce him," giggled Sundell. Laughter echoed around the room from all the boys, including Cimarron. Even Gage found his own actions to be amusing.

"Stop making me laugh so hard. It hurts too much to laugh!" replied Cimarron.

Nevada looked over at Smokey, who had a big grin on his face also. He smiled back at Smokey. *Well, now,* he thought. Things seemed to be getting back to normal as his boys were harassing each other again. This is the way he liked things to be when everybody was bonding with each other.

"Okay, listen up, everybody. We are all going home in the morning, except for TJ and Cimarron. TJ, you stay here until Cimarron is able to ride and see that he gets back to the ranch safely. The rest of us are heading home. We got to get the branding done and get that last cattle drive set up to move out to Denver. You two boys take your time coming home. Be careful, and we'll see you two when we get back home from Denver."

"Okay, Pa," said TJ. "I'll take good care of Cimarron."

"That's what I'm afraid of," voiced Cimarron. "Take him with you, Pa. I can get back home by myself."

"You'll take orders and go home with your brother, Cimarron. You're not going home alone with bandages on your head and chest. Now you'll take my orders and like it."

"Aw, Pa. I'll be fine."

"You'll both be fine. Say your good-byes tonight, boys, because we are leaving early in the morning. We'll see you two boys when we all get back home again."

~~~**T2**~~~

Early the next morning, Nevada, Smokey, Sundell, Ty, and Gage left to return home to the ranch in Yuma, Arizona. Nevada did exactly as the sheriff told him and did not say good-bye to the sheriff or anybody. They just slipped out of town quietly and were on their way, heading out to the Bitter End Trail and the long ride back home.

Silently sitting on the bedside table next to Cimarron was a new package of genuine Bull Durham chewing tobacco left there by Nevada, when he peeked in that morning before he left, as he checked up on his sleeping boys.

~~~**T2**~~~

A knock on the door at ten in the morning woke up the late-sleeping boys.

"Who is it?" inquired TJ.

"It's Jesse Russell and Janice," came the reply back.

"Okay. Wait a minute," replied TJ. He hurried and pulled on his jeans, then hustled to open the door with no shirt, socks, or boots on. Cimarron was stirring a little bit but still sleeping. "C'mon in, folks," whispered TJ.

They walked into the room and saw that Cimarron was still sleeping.

"I see your family left town already. There were only two horses with the T2 Brand on them in the corral at the livery stable," said Jesse.

"Yes, sir. They left early this morning," replied TJ. "The doc says Cimarron cannot ride for another three days. I'm staying with him until Doc releases him and says he can make the ride back."

"We brought you boys some home-cooked food. There's fried chicken in the basket and a peach pie for your lunch. Hope you like it," said Jesse.

"Jesse, Janice, we don't know how to thank you enough for all you have done. Especially Janice. You saved my brother's life," said TJ.

"You're welcome, TJ. Your brother was worth saving. I wish I could have done more for him while we were in that back storage room. All I could do was keep the swelling down on his head until you got there. I knew you would all find your way there eventually."

"Doc says that's what saved his life. He was a lucky son of a gun. Tell you what, Janice. Cimarron owes you a well-trained barrel horse for free. I'll see that he gets you one and trains it properly."

"Thank you, TJ. But that is really not necessary. I'm just glad that he is okay."

"No. He will owe you one, if I have to deck his hide and make him do it. You'll see, girl. He owes you a lot, ma'am."

"Thank you, TJ. You are very thoughtful."

"Janice, you can stay here and visit if you like. I have an errand to do down at the bank. I'll meet you in an hour at the general store. So long, son." Jesse shook hands with TJ and left the room.

As soon as Jesse was out of earshot and gone, TJ pulled up a chair for Janice to sit down on. "I'd like to take you out for dinner tomorrow night, Janice." He sat down on his single bed and proceeded to put on his socks and boots.

"Oh. Do you think Cimarron will be well enough to eat out?"

"Not him, Janice. Just you and me. Kinda like a date. I'll see that he gets fed before we go out. He will be fine."

"If you're sure he will be okay, then I accept."

"Great! I'll pick you up in a buggy around six o'clock."

"Okay, TJ. I'll be ready," replied Janice.

TJ stood up and was putting on his shirt and buttoning it up just as Cimarron was beginning to stir and wake up. Cimarron was turning over on his side when he let out an expletive.

"Fuck! These ribs hurt."

"Watch your mouth, Cimarron. There's a lady present," warned TJ.

As I opened my eyes, there was Janice Russell sitting next to my bed, staring down at me. *Where the hell did she come from?* I thought.

"So sorry, Miss Janice, I didn't know anyone else was in the room. Somebody didn't have enough sense to wake me and warn me."

"Because I wanted you to sleep as long as you could. You need the rest, little brother."

"It's okay, Cimarron. You are forgiven," replied Janice.

"The least you could've done was straighten out my blankets so I'm covered up and looking decent, TJ, you dummy."

"I figured you always like looking like hell anyway. So I left you in your natural rumpled state. Ha ha ha!"

"Thanks a lot, big brother. You're a really nice guy. Did Pa leave yet?"

"He's gone, Cimarron. They left early this morning. I'll comb your hair and shave you before breakfast. Right now, I think a thank-you is in order for Janice saving your life."

"Yes, ma'am. TJ's right. I almost forgot. Thank you very much, ma'am, for all you did for me. They told me how you took care of me. I'm grateful, ma'am."

"You're welcome, Cimarron. I'm glad I was able to help."

"Cimarron, I told Janice you owe her a barrel racing horse, and y'all will train it for her free of charge. What do ya say about that?"

"You sure enough got that right! I'll take care of it for you just as soon as I get back to the ranch and get working again, Janice. You got my promise on that, ma'am."

"Thank you, Cimarron. That is swell of you. Well, I guess I better get going. My Pa will be waiting for me."

Janice stood up and bent over, kissing Cimarron on the lips, and he responded by kissing her back. TJ noticed how Cimarron's face glowed and how he melted with that kiss, making TJ a little bit jealous.

"Okay, little brother. You stay put while I walk Janice downstairs and outside. I'll get you some breakfast and be back to take care of you."

"Don't take too much time about it, TJ. I'm checking the watch," Cimarron mumbled as TJ went out the door behind Janice. Laughing with a big smile on his face as he left the room, TJ flipped off Cimarron with a discouraging hand sign behind his back for only Cimarron to see before he closed the room door.

Well, that no-good son of a gun, I thought, as my big brother left me alone and in pain. For an attorney, he shows no respect for me at all. I timed, on the watch, how long my brother was gone, and it was about an hour before he came back. At least he had breakfast for me when he returned, because I was starving.

"How are you doing, Cimarron? I brought you a nice breakfast. Eat, and then I'll help you get up, get shaved, and get dressed. I saw Jennifer at the café, and she is coming up to see you later."

"You were gone long enough. What took you so long?"

"I treated Janice to breakfast at the café. It was nice and cozy, I might add. Just the two of us. That's when I ran into Jennifer. I told her she could visit you in about an hour. So eat your breakfast, and then I'll get you cleaned up, shaved, and dressed. Do you think you can sit up in bed?"

"Damn right, I'll sit up. Just give me a hand."

My brother helped me sit up, and he put the breakfast plate on my lap. It wasn't long before I made short work of the huevos rancheros and hot salsa. Then he helped me sit on the edge of the bed and brought over a pan of water and lye soap. I washed up, and TJ helped me get my jeans and a shirt on. I needed help with my socks and boots because my ribs were pretty darn sore. Then TJ got me out of bed and sat me in a chair. He shaved me and gently combed my hair around the bandages and stitches. Now I was feeling like my old self again, even though my ribs were really sore. I still had a dull ache in my head, but that should settle down when Doc takes the stitches out tomorrow. I tried to stand up but got dizzy and almost fell. Good thing TJ was there to catch me and sit me back down.

"You can't get up and walk around today, little brother. I'll walk you around tomorrow when the stitches are out, and you get some more strength back."

There was a knock on the door, and TJ opened it up and let Jennifer in. The next thing I knew, she was sitting on my lap, in the chair, hugging me, and I was wincing and trying to hold back the sounds of pain.

"Whoa, Jennifer. You can't sit on him. He has three broken ribs. Take it easy on him, girl," said TJ as he started to grab for her to take her off me.

"Leave her there," I said. "She is on my lap now. Just don't move around, Jennifer. Stay still in one spot." She started kissing me like crazy, and it was sure feeling as sweet as heaven in between my shots of pain. TJ placed a chair down next to mine and took her off my lap, plopping her on the chair next to me. Whew!

"Sit there, Jennifer. You don't want to hurt him any worse than he is, or I'll be stuck here with him longer than I want to be. I got a ranch to run, and we got to leave in another day.

"Oh no. You are leaving so soon?" replied Jennifer.

"Yes. Day after tomorrow. As soon as the doc says Cimarron can ride."

"Oh, honey, I'll miss you. You can't leave so soon."

There was a knock on the door. It was the deputy from the sheriff's office. "Sheriff wants to see you," he said to TJ when TJ answered the door.

"Okay. Tell him I'll be right there. Jennifer, you probably should leave now. Cimarron needs to rest."

"No. I'm not ready to go yet. I'll go when you get back from the sheriff's office. Somebody should stay with him. By the time you get back, I'll have to report to work at the saloon."

I saw the disturbed look on TJ's face. No way in hell did he want to leave me alone with her. She would climb all over me as soon as he left us alone. Not that I would mind, but I wasn't exactly in shape for that kind of entertainment. TJ gave me his look of authority, but he left the room much against his better judgment.

~~~T2~~~

When TJ arrived at the sheriff's office, he was quite surprised by what Sheriff Williams had to say. It seems that Cullen and Ace were wanted dead or alive by the law up in northern Arizona territory, and the sheriff handed TJ the reward of two thousand dollars in cash for the capture of the outlaws. The paperwork for the bank just came in over the wire. Sheriff Williams said the town council decided that the Lacey family deserved to receive the reward because we cleaned out a nasty den of outlaws that were plaguing the area for some time. TJ was thrilled to take the money and recoup the loss our ranch experienced, with an extra five hundred dollars to boot. He couldn't wait to get back and tell me I wouldn't have to work for him and the ranch for forty years with no pay! I was back on the thirty-dollar-a-month payroll again. Yahoo! He was surprised to see that Jennifer was gone when he walked into our hotel room.

"So where did the girl go?" inquired TJ.

"Oh. She had to go to work, so she left ten minutes ago."

"Why didn't she take her lipstick with her?" asked TJ.

"What do you mean?" I said.

"She left it all over your face, and I just shaved that face for you. Some women have no class at all," laughed TJ, shaking his head. He handed me a hand mirror and a soapy rag from the bowl of water on the side table. I washed everything but the smirk off my face.

"I ain't complainin'," I said.

"No. You wouldn't, little brother. Where's your money belt?"

"Pa put it in the drawer of the side table," I said. TJ pulled out this big wad of money and showed it to me, then put it in the money belt and strapped the belt around his waist, under his shirt, and tucked his shirt back in. "Where did that come from?" I said.

"Two thousand dollars. The sheriff gave us the reward money for two of those outlaws that were wanted," said TJ.

About all I could do was whistle. I couldn't jump up and down because everything hurt too much, especially after Jennifer's generous attentions.

"You're back on the payroll again, little brother."

"Pa said I was never off it!"

"Yeah. That's what Pa said, but I figured differently. I planned on taking it out of your hide for being so careless, just as soon as you were well again," laughed TJ.

"You're kidding me, right?"

"Yeah, right, Cimarron," TJ giggled again. "You think between the two of us, we can get this bankroll back home safely to Yuma?" He patted his stomach.

"No sweat, big brother. We'll do it, all right."

TJ got me out of bed the next day and walked me back and forth. My strength was coming back, and I was feeling pretty good. The doc stopped by and checked me out again and said I was good to go and travel the trail back to Yuma tomorrow. Nobody was happier than me to get out of this town and get my life back to normal again on the ranch. All the pretty girls in the world couldn't hold me here any longer. I took the lives away from two cowboys in this here town, and I wanted to get the hell out before the sheriff or anybody else decided to change their minds on letting me go. The sooner I get out of here, the better I'll feel. The odds of surviving the wilderness of the Bitter End Trail were much higher than staying in this worthless town of Brawley waiting to possibly get my neck stretched.

TJ recognized my restlessness and knew immediately that I was ready to take off. He wasted no time packing our gear and having everything ready to move out early in the morning. Then he took off and disappeared for most of the evening. He thought I didn't know he was going on a date with Janice Russell. I knew what he was up to the minute he got done shaving and borrowed my scent from my saddlebags and splashed his face with it. I didn't know what their plans included, and I didn't ask. I do know that he was gone for a long time. When he slipped in late that night, I was awake and heard him. He fell asleep within five minutes. Hell, he must have had a very busy, trying night. Damn, if he ain't one ahead of me again. I rolled over and went back to sleep and slept sound until morning.

CHAPTER X

BACK TRAIL TO HOME

"Cimarron, you got ten minutes to get your jeans on, that fly buttoned up, and your boots on. I'm going to saddle our horses for the trip back home."

"Ten minutes? I need at least an hour to say good-bye to Jennifer. Ten minutes is nothing to say good-bye to a girl."

"Ten minutes. Be ready when I get back. Say good-bye with your pants on. You already had two days to say good-bye to her," said TJ.

"But, TJ, I was in pain and agony for two days. How could I say good-bye to her in the condition I was in with three broken ribs? You don't have any heart at all."

"Who do you think you're kidding, little brother? I saw you milking that condition and getting all her sympathy. You got to get up earlier than that to fool me. I've known you your whole life, little brother. Don't think I don't know when you are performing for the sake of a woman's attention. Ha ha ha! Be ready in ten minutes. I'll help you get down the stairs and on your horse. You got to leave the tape and those bandages under your shirt. Remember, the tape has got to stay on really tight, or those injured ribs will hurt on the trail ride back home. Okay?"

"Hell, yeah. I hear you. But I've been busted up worse 'n this, taking the pitch out of stallions. Ten minutes is ridiculous. Take your time saddling those mounts, big brother."

"*Ten minutes*," said TJ again, and he closed the door behind him as he left the room with a big smirk on his face, shaking his head.

Jennifer was knocking at the door shortly after TJ left. Cimarron let her in, encircled his arms around her, and said, "We got ten minutes to say good-bye, darlin'. Maybe less than that."

"Ten minutes? That's nothing to say good-bye to a cowboy."

"I know, darlin'. That's what I told my big brother. But my brother, TJ, will be back here shortly to help me down the stairs and onto my horse. He's giving me ten minutes, and that's all."

"You always let your brother run your life? That's not fair."

"Sorry, darlin'. You got to understand that no man is my master. I swallow my hardships and complaints like I swallow my coffee. I ride for the T2 Ranch Brand. TJ is ten years older than me, and I work for him because he is one of the owners and bosses on our spread. I got to take his orders. I'm just one of the thirty-dollar-a-month cowhands on the spread. So now, I want a really nice kiss from you. None of these short, little pecks 'cause that ain't gonna cut it. Mmm, darlin'. Give me some more of that nice sugar."

TJ intruded into the room, interrupting that long kiss. "Okay, break it up. Time's up. Let's go, *Romeo*. Pick up your gear, and I'll help you down the stairs."

"His name is Cimarron, not Romeo. Don't you even know your own brother's name?" said Jennifer in frustrated anger.

"I know his name. I'm just teasing him is all. Romeo is a character in the opera, who is a lover boy. Have you ever been to an opera house back East, Jennifer?" replied TJ.

"No. Of course not. Why would I want to go back East and know who this Romeo is?"

"C'mon, Cimarron. Let's move out of this town. We're wasting time jawing. I don't want you upsetting the law in this town and staying longer than you should. Put your arm around my shoulder."

"Bye, Jennifer darlin'. I'll look you up next time I'm in town, honey."

"Bye, Cimarron. Have a safe trip home, sweetheart."

"Watch your step on these stairs, Cimarron. I'll give you as much support as I can, but if you slip and fall, I won't be able catch you or hold on to you."

"All right, just go slow. Hey, TJ. I got to get my ass back to this town again really soon. I told Jennifer I'd be back to see her."

"This town doesn't want you, Cimarron. You killed two Double D Bar ranch hands here with your fast draw."

"They were outlaws. I did Brawley a favor."

"I don't think the sheriff or the townsfolk appreciated it, outlaws or not. They should have been locked up and gotten a fair trial. Outlaws have rights too, you know."

"That's the way attorneys think, TJ. You got too much book learning in you. This town is the way the real world is, and people got to live in it, regardless of your so-called laws. Thanks to me, they can now live in it without fear of being robbed."

"I'm not going to argue right or wrong with you, little brother, because we aren't in a courtroom." Cimarron just looked at his brother and snickered and shook his head. *Now we need to be in a courtroom to have an argument. Jeez.*

~~~T2~~~

They rode back across the Bitter End Trail at a gentle, easy lope so as not to jar Cimarron's broken ribs, which would cause too much pain. They chatted as they walked the horses along the narrow trail.

"That girl Janice was a nice girl," said TJ.

"She was really pretty, all right," said Cimarron. "But too permanent, if you ask me. I like Jennifer better. No commitments."

"What do you mean 'too permanent'?" questioned TJ.

"She was the marrying kind."

"So what's wrong with the marrying kind?" said TJ.

"I'm not ready to be tied down to matrimonial ropes yet. I'm still having fun."

"Well, I am, and from where I was looking, Janice was fine enough for me."

"Suit yourself, big brother. She sure is pretty though when she gets her dander up. Cute as a button with that temper," said Cimarron. "The cowboy that marries her though will have a hell of a time keeping her from stumbling all over herself and falling on folks. Ha ha ha! Hey, TJ. Did I ever tell you the story about the time I took that order for four stallions to the town of Brotherhood, California? There was this girl there, and she had the biggest, uh, personality . . ."

"No, Cimarron. You never told me that story. I got a good feeling though that I'm about to hear it."

Book Six Summary

RIDING JUDGMENT TRAIL

(Sundell Lacey's Story)

I opened my eyes to the flickering of the sunshine on them, and the only thing I knew was that I had a gosh-awful bad headache. My pillow was a large boulder, so whatever happened, I realized I must have hit my head on the rock it was resting on when I fell—if that is what happened, if I fell.

I moved my arms, and they seemed to be fine; no pain there. When I moved my legs, they felt quite stiff; however, they loosened up and moved freely and seemed to be okay also. No broken bones in my extremities. I sat up, and my head began to spin and reel like a child's toy top. I held on to some rocks jutting out of the wall next to me. The spinning and reeling slowed down and stopped. My back seemed to be okay, a little sore from the fall, but it too was okay with a few sore muscles at the most.

When I looked to my left side, all I could see was the rock wall of a mountain going straight up. It's when I looked to my right side that I shot the cat over the ledge and lost almost everything that was in my belly from the day before. I was sitting on a ledge that jutted out on the side of a mountain. I looked at the rock where my head was, and it had blood on it. When I felt my head, there was dry blood on it where I hit it.

How I got on this ledge, I had no clue, and this ledge looked to be forty feet in the air above a ravine. There would be no climbing back up that rock wall to the trail above; it was way too steep. My best bet to get off this mountain ledge was to climb down it to what looked like a trail below and a meandering brook or river alongside that trail. There was no question about it; I had to get down to that trail and get a drink in that brook if I wanted to survive.

That's when I saw the dead horse at the bottom of the ravine. The horse must be mine, and we must have fallen off that mountain trail from up above. I must have landed on this ledge, which saved my life, but my horse didn't live through the fall. The buzzards were already circling around him.

My saddle, my gear, and everything I owned were on that dead horse, and the buzzards were ready to dive out of the sky and devour the animal. I had no choice but to climb down the side of this mountain and get to my stuff. Whatever I could salvage was important for my survival.

Printed in the United States
By Bookmasters